KU-034-500

Nick's October

Nick took his coffee into the sitting-room and perched on the table. Yes, he reflected, being twenty-one was the beginning of the end. That's why Mature People were so keen to celebrate it. Join the Crumblies Club, son. Welcome aboard.

He picked up the pot of paint and, in huge Spring Mist letters, painted SENILITY STARTS AT 21 across Maurice's green wall. He stirred his coffee and surveyed the large statement. He rather liked it.

Also available from Methuen Teens

I'm Not Your Other Half by Caroline B. Cooney
The Changeover by Margaret Mahy
Fire and Hemlock by Diana Wynne Jones
Haunted by Judith St George
The Teenagers' Handbook by Peter Murphy and Kitty Grime

By the same author in Magnet Books

The Ghost Within
Haunted Children
Goodbye Summer

Nick's October

ALISON PRINCE

Methuen

First published 1986
by Methuen Children's Books Ltd
This Methuen Teens paperback edition first published 1987
by Methuen Children's Books Ltd
11 New Fetter Lane, London EC4P 4EE
Copyright © 1986 Alison Prince
Printed in Great Britain by
Richard Clay Ltd, Bungay, Suffolk

ISBN 0 416 06252 0

This paperback is sold subject to the condition
that it shall not, by way of trade or otherwise,
be lent, re-sold, hired out or otherwise circulated
without the publisher's prior consent in any form of
binding or cover other than that in which it is
published and without a similar condition
including this condition being imposed
on the subsequent purchaser

Chapter 1

Nick sprawled in front of the television with his head propped on one arm of the sofa and his feet on the other.

'A History of Warfare', the screen proclaimed in letters made of swords for the straight lines and scimitars for the curved ones. A hairy creature hit another one over the head with a large stone and then they both disappeared in the mushroom cloud of a nuclear explosion and the name of the author of the series.

Nick groaned. 'I suppose you want to watch all this crud,' he said.

'Yes, I bloody do,' agreed Maurice. 'And we'll have none of your smart comments. There's a couple of cans of beer in the kitchen. You can have one if it'll help you shut up.'

'No, thanks,' said Nick. He knew what it would mean if he accepted the beer. Sooner or later, the mean old devil would remind him of it. 'You live in my flat, eat my food, drink my beer . . . .' Never mind that Nick chipped in every week.

'Suit yourself,' said his father.

A black and white documentary film flickered across the screen. First World War trenches, men floundering towards barbed wire entanglements. A sea of mud.

'Why do they wear those bandage-things on their legs?' asked Nick. 'They all got sprained ankles or something?'

'Puttees,' said Maurice. 'Kept the rats from running up your trousers.'

'Don't know why they did it,' said Nick with distaste.

'Oh, rats know where it's warm and dry,' said his father knowledgeably.

'No, you daft old prat, why those blokes went out there and fought,' said Nick. 'It was all for nothing, anyway. Nobody *won* the stupid war.'

5

'What do you mean?' demanded Maurice. '*We* won it.'

'There was an Armistice,' Nick corrected. 'The Germans decided to pack it in. We did it at school, in History.'

Maurice gestured angrily at the screen and said, 'My father was in that lot somewhere. If it hadn't been for him and men like him, you might not be here, boy.'

'Don't be stupid,' said Nick tiredly. 'Look at all those corpses on the wire. *They* didn't go home and get their wives pregnant, did they? Nobody's here because of them. If your old man hadn't kept his head down, *you* wouldn't have been born, either, and nor would I. Fighting's stupid. They'd all have been better staying here and minding their own business.'

'You make me sick,' said Maurice. His pale blue eyes bulged in his red face and the lank strands of his hair dangled as if it, too, was sick. 'You know what happened to men who wouldn't go over the top when the whistle blew? They were shot by their own officers, and quite right, too. That's the sort of thing we need these days. Discipline.'

'You're off your bloody head,' said Nick. He got to his feet and added, 'I'm going out.'

'Scared you might learn something,' said Maurice, watching with grim intensity as a hand grenade landed in a foxhole where a group of German soldiers had been sheltering.

'No risk of that with you,' said Nick bitterly. 'You think you know it all.' He shut the door behind him quickly, to cut off his father's shouted reply, and grabbed his leather jacket from the row of pegs by the front door. Then he picked up his crash helmet and went out.

From the twelfth-floor balcony outside the flat, buildings stretched away to the river in a pattern of rectangles, tall blocks studded with windows, some dark, some lit from inside in the early autumn evening. Far below, street lights already shone orange, and a woman walked her dog across the open space where, Nick knew, the notices on the walls said 'No Ball Games'. From long habit, he stared down through the glass to where his Kawasaki stood parked among the cars. It was still there. A nightmare lurked at the back of his mind that one day it would be gone. Bikes got stolen every day of the week, but there was nothing he could do about it. Gary had said he could put the Kawa in the shed behind his place, but it was a bus ride to Gary's, and that meant hassle and expense. And who said life was safe, anyway?

Not bothering to wait for the lift, Nick pushed open the heavy door at the end of the balcony and started down the stairs, to and fro down their zig-zagging flights. The walls were rich with spray-can inscriptions and the smell of urine became stronger as he neared the ground floor. Nick went out across the linking bridge to the next block, and down the open steps to the street.

Then he stopped.

Two boys were investigating his bike, one stooping to look at the tyres, the other half-seated on the saddle, hand on the throttle twist-grip as he leaned forward to examine the figure on the mileometer. Furtively, Nick shifted his hold on the crash helmet to grasp it firmly by its face-bar. Adrenalin rose in him as he walked quietly towards the bike, making him feel short of breath. It was difficult to keep his heels on the ground, so violent was the desire to leap at these intruders. The bike was his, not theirs. Part of him.

The boy sitting on the saddle glanced up and saw him. 'Come on!' he said urgently, and ran. The boy crouched by the back wheel was a little slower to get away, and Nick flung himself across the bike and aimed a ferocious blow at him with the crash helmet, catching him on the hip. The boy staggered and almost fell, but recovered himself and followed his friend in a crouching run. They ducked behind the pillars under the flats and disappeared round the corner of the block where the lift-shaft was.

Nick glared after them. Then he inspected the bike carefully. It did not seem to have been damaged. He straddled it and put on his crash helmet, then fished in his pocket for the keys and fitted them in the ignition. He kicked the stand up with his left foot and started the engine, then circled slowly under the flats as he looked in vain for any sight of the boys. Then he came back past the line of parked cars, braked for the T-junction at the end of the narrow street, and turned left into the main road.

His fury ebbed in the pleasure of riding. The Kawa's quick response was deeply satisfying, and Nick thought with contempt of his father sitting before the television in the stuffy room, avidly watching the scenes of war. And yet, as he wove his way through the traffic, Nick saw as if through the eyes of an outsider, the blow he had aimed at the fleeing boy. He wondered whether war could produce the same fury against people who were merely playing for the other team. He paused momentarily at traffic lights, revved the engine as he saw the traffic come to a halt on the other side of the junction, and was away on the amber before the cars had got any kind of start. The burst of speed brought its unfailing excitement, and Nick felt angry again with the intruders. The thought of anyone else interfering with this intensely personal machine was painful.

He turned into the tree-lined street where Sasha lived, and pulled up on the right-hand side of the road, outside her house. The sound of a piano came from the front room, and Sasha's bedroom light was on. She wouldn't have gone to bed, though. Since her father had left last year, Sasha had been spending a lot of time on her own upstairs, while her mother played the sad old waltz tunes Nick now recognised as Chopin. He heaved the bike on to its centre stand because of the downhill camber on its right, then walked up the garden path and rang the bell, twice.

Sasha's mother played on. She was used to Nick's ring now, and ignored it. Through the sunset-shaped pebble glass of the front door, Nick saw a pale pattern of broken spots approaching, which was Sasha coming downstairs. She opened the door and kissed him, then said, 'Come in.' He followed her into the kitchen.

'Coffee?' asked Sasha.

'Wouldn't mind,' said Nick.

He looked at Sasha appreciatively as she filled the kettle. Her hair had been pink when he first knew her, but now she had bleached it blonde. She wore a dress which seemed to be a patchwork of different creamy-coloured materials, some plain and some scattered with small pinkish flowers. He nodded at it and said, 'That's nice.'

Sasha turned to him, glowing. 'Do you like it?' she said

8

eagerly. 'I hoped you would.'

As always, Nick was faintly embarrassed by her intensity. 'It's all right,' he said, refusing to be stampeded. 'Did you make it?'

'Yes, the Abrahams gave me a whole pile of off-cuts and I turned them into this,' said Sasha. 'It was a sort of consolation prize, I think. I've been doing button holes all week, and they're awful, specially in a loosely-woven tweed.' She looked at him and added, 'What's the matter? You look cross. Have you been quarrelling with your father again?'

Nick remembered his original reason for leaving the flat. He hitched himself on to the work surface beside the Kenwood and started to roll a cigarette. 'He's such a stupid old bugger,' he said. 'Sits there watching these old war films and going on about "Young People Today". I don't know why he's like that, wanting things all dead organised. It'd be worse than school.'

'And that was bad enough,' agreed Sasha. She spooned instant coffee into two mugs and poured in boiling water, then stirred thoughtfully. 'Mum's a bit like that,' she said. 'When she's talking at all, that is. Most of the time she just goes around looking stricken.'

'Tell me something new,' said Nick. He hoped Sasha was not going to start a long moan about her mother. There was no point in escaping from Maurice just to get dragged into talking about someone else's crazy parents.

'Oh, all right,' said Sasha a little irritably. 'You don't want to know. Must you make it so blatantly obvious?'

Nick did not answer. He contemplated jumping off the work-top and walking out.

'Sorry,' said Sasha. 'I know — you're allergic to being bawled out.'

Nick shrugged, relenting a bit. After all, he thought, Mrs Bowman couldn't have been much fun to live with in these months since her husband left. 'Still walking around like Lady Macbeth, is she?' he asked.

'Oh, worse,' said Sasha, handing Nick his coffee. 'Lady Em just had the heebies because she kept murdering people, but Mum's sort of — martyred.'

9

'She ought to get a job,' said Nick. 'Take her mind off it. I mean, he's been gone nearly a year now.'

'Oh, get a job, just like that!' said Sasha with irony. 'You'd been unemployed for months when I first met you, Dominic Alexander Cartwright! And Mum's fifty-one, and hasn't worked for years. Who's going to consider *her* for a job?'

'She's a qualified teacher, *Susan Bowman*,' Nick reminded her. Two could play at this proper names business.

'Oh, all right,' said Sasha again. 'She's a qualified music teacher, yes, but there aren't many music jobs about, not the way things are now. Schools don't have money for that sort of thing.'

Nick sipped his coffee. This conversation was depressing, he thought. 'I was talking to a bloke with a Renault 4 at the garage the other day,' he said. 'He reckoned we ought to have a revolution in this country, same as they did in Russia. October 1917, he said. Power to the people. Could be right.'

Sasha laughed. 'You see, you're just like your father at heart,' she said. 'You'd join an army all right if it was fighting for something you liked the idea of. You'd go out and kill people.'

'I wouldn't just because I was *told* to,' Nick objected. 'And I'd never fight people just because they happened to belong to some other country.' Sasha had caught him on the wrong foot, and he felt confused. He regretted mentioning what the stupid bloke had said. And yet, inwardly, he knew what he meant. 'Having a lot of money doesn't make people better than the rest of us,' he said. 'We all matter just as much as anyone else. You have to find out what it is you can do, that's all. Then do it.'

'Yes,' said Sasha. 'I know what you mean.'

'That's why people like my dad have got the wrong idea,' Nick ploughed on. 'It's so stupid to think we need tougher rules. If other people make rules for you, you're so busy fighting them that you can't start making your own rules. And that's what you've got to do, really.'

'Motor bikes for everyone?' queried Sasha, grinning. 'And —'

'No,' said Nick impatiently. 'My rules wouldn't be for you, or

10

for anyone else. They'd just be for me. If I could get it together.'

Sasha looked at him mockingly over the rim of her coffee mug. 'So this is Nick's October revolution, is it?' she said. 'You'll have to hurry up. It's September now. You've only got a month to get it planned.'

Nick shook his head, exasperated. Then he became aware that the sound of the piano in the sitting-room had stopped. He gave Sasha a warning glance and she, like him, turned to look expectantly at the door.

Sasha's mother somehow managed to make the whole room seem tense before she came into it, Nick thought. He got a smile ready for the white-faced presence and switched it on as Joanna Bowman opened the kitchen door and stood resentfully in the doorway.

'You don't have to stop talking when I come in,' she said.

'We didn't, Mum,' Sasha assured her. 'You just hit a natural pause.'

'Yeah,' Nick agreed. He tried to remind himself that he ought to feel sorry for Mrs Bowman. She did not look at him as she went towards the kettle, leaning her hand on the edge of the sink and then on the draining-board as she made her way past them. She gave the impression that it hurt to move.

'What you been doing, then,' he ventured, trying to be pleasant. 'Getting in lots of piano practice?'

Joanna gave a short, unamused laugh. 'I would hardly call it practice,' she said. 'To practise, one needs an objective.' She sighed, weighed the kettle in her hand to see if it contained enough water, and switched it on. 'But it passes the time,' she added.

The kettle, already hot, boiled at once, and Nick saw Mrs Bowman glance with a trace of reproach at Sasha's coffee mug as she made some for herself. Sasha saw it, too.

'We didn't think you'd want to be disturbed,' she said, 'or we'd have brought you some.'

'Yes,' said her mother on a faint sigh.

They all sipped their coffee in an uneasy silence. Nick toyed with the idea of suggesting to Sasha that they might go up to

11

her room, and abandoned it. Mrs Bowman knew perfectly well that he stayed the night quite often, but knowing it, for her, was not the same as being able to talk about it. Nick thought it was no wonder Sasha's old man had shoved off. He couldn't imagine Mrs B as being much of a turn-on in bed. For some reason, his mind darted back to early childhood as he remembered averting a screwed-up face from the licked hanky wielded by his own mother. But at least she'd been pretty, not like this woman with her limp, colourless hair still worn little-girl style in an Alice band. They used to go down the market, and some of the stallholders would whistle, and shout suggestions which Nick hadn't understood at the time. And Barbie would shout cheerful abuse back, and slap half-heartedly at the grubby hands which reached out for her as she argued about the price of apples. Perhaps he'd go and look her up, Nick thought, her and Tim in Croydon. Must be months since he'd seen them. Not that he felt guilty about it. Barbie and Tim didn't need anyone else. Best of luck to them.

Joanna looked out of the window and said distantly, 'Some woman came to ask if I'd play for a ballet class.'

'Great,' said Nick, but his comment was lost in Sasha's enthusiastic response. '*Really*? Oh, Mum, that's marvellous!'

'I don't know,' said Joanna, still staring at the darkening garden. 'It's in Southfields. Such an awkward journey.'

'But you've got the car,' Sasha protested.

Her mother did not reply. After a pause, she said, 'All those awful little girls.'

Nick saw the quick rise of colour to Sasha's face and groaned inwardly. There was going to be a row.

'Look, Mum,' Sasha said, 'it's no use just sitting here and *festering*. I know it's been difficult, these last months – it has for me, too, but – '

'No, it hasn't,' said her mother flatly. 'You've been enjoying it. Going over to Richmond to see your father and his woman whenever you feel like it. You were the one who pushed him into it in the first place. You could have left things as they were, but no. Once you found out about Laura, you had to make everyone do what you thought was right. Never mind who got hurt.'

'You can't *make* people do things,' Nick pointed out.

Joanna looked at him with loathing. 'You always put your oar in, don't you?' she said. 'Susan would never have behaved as she did if it hadn't been for your influence.'

'That's not fair!' protested Sasha. 'And I do wish you wouldn't call me Susan.'

'It *is* your name,' said her mother bleakly. 'Yes, I know. You changed it. You're good at changing things, aren't you. People managed to live their lives for a good few years before you started reforming them, you know. They were even happy, in their inefficient way. But that isn't good enough for Susan Bowman. *Sasha* Bowman,' she corrected herself bitterly. 'Oh, no. Everything's got to fit in with *her* standards.'

Nick put down his half-full mug and got off the work-top. 'Thanks for the coffee,' he said. 'See you.'

'Oh, Nick, don't go!' begged Sasha.

'You're not allowed to go,' said her mother sarcastically. 'It's not in the Sasha Bowman scheme of things.'

Nick picked up his crash helmet. 'I can see why David left,' he said, and walked out.

Sasha ran after him to the front door. 'Look, it's not *my* fault,' she said. 'I know she's awful. But it's me you're leaving, not her.'

'Can't handle it,' said Nick. 'Too much hassle. I'll see you.'

Sasha put her arms round his neck and kissed him. 'I do love you,' she said. 'I'm sorry things are such a mess.'

'Yeah,' said Nick. 'I know.' She smelt wonderful. He cursed Mrs Bowman mentally. Sasha was right. It wasn't her fault. From behind the closed kitchen door he could hear the muffled sound of her mother sobbing. 'Best if I go,' he said more gently. 'See you tomorrow, right? I'll try and get round early.'

Sasha nodded, downcast, and the blonde curls bobbed disconsolately. Nick put his finger under her chin to lift her head, and kissed her. 'Cheer up, Lolly-top,' he said. It was the name he had used for her months ago, when her hair had been pink. Sasha smiled bravely. 'Okay,' she said.

Nick buckled on his crash helmet as he walked down the path

to the bike and heaved it off its stand. He started the engine and glanced back. Sasha was still standing at the door. Faintly irritated by this clinging fidelity, Nick found a pet phrase of his father's echoing in his mind. 'You want to remember, boy, if you fancy a girl, look at her mother first. They always turn out like their mothers.'

But then, Nick thought, the old git was wrong about most things. He was probably wrong about that, too. He raised a hand in farewell, and rode off.

Chapter 2

Maurice was still sitting in front of the television when Nick got back. He glanced up and said, 'That was a quick one.'

'Oh, shut up,' said Nick. He slumped down in a chair. On the screen, a car slewed round a corner, rolled and burst into flames.

'I was thinking,' said his father, 'it's coming up to your twenty-first.'

Nick made no answer. It was his birthday on Sunday week, as Sasha kept reminding him. He wished everyone would just forget it.

'I mean,' said Maurice, 'it only happens once.'

'So does every day,' said Nick. 'Thank God.'

'You don't make things easy, do you?' said Maurice irritably.

Nick shrugged. If the old boy was working his way round to asking what he wanted for his birthday, he thought, a pair of gauntlets would come in handy. His old ones had a split inside each thumb, and the wind fairly whistled through.

'No, I thought we ought to have a bit of a do,' Maurice went on. 'Ask a few friends in. Family.'

'Family!' Nick gave a yelp of laughter. 'What family?'

'There's Walter and Enid,' Maurice suggested.

'Oh, yes,' said Nick sarcastically. 'Own about twenty

14

fish-and-chip shops and run a BMW each. They're *really* likely to come, aren't they? I hope they don't, anyway. They were at Auntie Alice's funeral, and poor old Ernie was really cut up about her dying, but Enid gave him a hard time about the sherry being South African. Bitch. Don't know how Mum came to have a sister like that.'

Maurice glared at him. 'If I say we're having a party, we're having a party,' he said.

'Whether I like it or not,' said Nick.

'That's right,' agreed his father.

' "Happy Birthday To You",' Nick sang as offensively as he could. ' "Happy Bir – " '

'*Shut up!*' bawled Maurice.

Nick draped his legs over the arm of his chair and closed his eyes, folding his arms.

Maurice got up and switched the television off. Then he sat down again. Nick watched him covertly. His father's stubby fingers plucked absently at the frayed edges of a hole in the chair's cover. After a few minutes, Maurice tried again. 'A twenty-first birthday,' he said, '– well, it's a kind of landmark. I'm not perfect, but I know what's the right thing to do. I've had it in mind for some time. I've asked a few people already, matter of fact. Terry said he'll come.'

Nick groaned. 'Not the cross-eyed Irishman? Who else? All the rest of the Plumbers' Arms' regulars, I suppose?'

'One or two of my mates, yes,' said Maurice with dignity. 'You can bring *your* friends.'

'Oh, ta,' said Nick. 'You've got it all planned, haven't you? Never mind if I want a party or not. It's the done thing to have a twenty-first party, so you're having one. Well, you can count me out.'

'You wouldn't do that,' said Maurice in alarm.

'Wouldn't I,' said Nick darkly. But he sighed inwardly. No, he wouldn't. He could see the whole ghastly event already, just as it was going to be. Women in their best dresses sipping Babycham and telling Maurice where he could get stretch covers for the chairs quite cheaply. Jam jars of Twiglets. The more he thought about it, the worse it seemed. They would have to

15

provide food. Not to mention booze. 'Who's going to pay for all this?' he asked.

'I been putting a bit by,' said Maurice. 'They got a club down the off-licence, you can pay in.' His chin stuck out obstinately.

Nick transferred his feet to the floor. He sat and looked at them for a minute, in their motor-cycle boots with the buckles dangling. Then he said, 'You don't have to, honest. These days, people don't expect it.'

'I don't care what people expect,' said his father. 'I know what's right.' He met Nick's eye. 'You're ashamed of this place, aren't you. Don't want people here.'

'No!' protested Nick.

'I'll clean it up,' Maurice assured him. 'Give the walls a coat of paint, maybe. I want to do something you'll remember. Once a kid's twenty-one he's grown up. It's what you might call the last time. I don't want to miss it. I missed a lot. Wish things had been different sometimes.'

'They've been okay,' said Nick awkwardly. Poor old bugger, he thought, he always mucks things up. Sasha had plans for a meal round at her house and God only knew what. She'd just have to forget it, that's all. 'What are you going to do about food?' he asked with a faint flicker of hope. Maybe his father hadn't thought about that. But Maurice smiled. 'I got the catering in hand,' he said. 'All in hand. You'll be surprised, boy.'

'Oh, bloody hell,' said Nick, getting up wearily. 'Okay. We're having a party. You want a cup of tea?'

'Wouldn't mind,' said his father. 'If you're making one.'

'I wouldn't ask if I wasn't,' retorted Nick, and went out to the kitchen. No good letting the old devil think he'd won too easily.

'Tea break,' said Gary, walking past Nick as he squatted beside an Escort, rubbing down the filler on the front wing. Nick dropped his bit of wet-and-dry back in the bucket and stood up, wiping his hands on his boiler-suit. He made his way round the hoist to the rear of the garage where Len, who owned the place, was already sitting at ground level in a seat which had come out of an old Triumph Herald, pulling the lid off his sandwich box.

Nick collected his Snoopy mug of tea from among those which stood around the Calor gas burner. On the wall behind it were a few tattered pin-ups and Len's collection of cards printed with witty sayings such as 'Be Alert. England Needs Lerts'. Nobody ever laughed at them, but Len added a new one from time to time, as if out of a sense of duty. Gary was sitting on the floor of a VW camper van whose sliding door stood open, his back propped comfortably against its rear seat.

'Shove over,' said Nick.

Gary moved his feet to make room. He always looked lost inside his overalls, which hung on his thin body like the baggy costume on a clown, and his ears stuck out at right-angles to his head under a wispy thatch of brown hair. He was eating cheese-and-onion crisps out of the packet. Nick reached over and took one.

'Buy your own, you greedy bugger,' said Gary, fending Nick off with a half-hearted elbow.

'Pay you back Sunday week,' said Nick, taking another. 'As many as you like. The old man's having a party.'

Gary choked slightly and his eyebrows shot up. 'He's *what?*' he asked.

'You heard,' said Nick gloomily. 'Supposed to be for my twenty-first.' The idea seemed even worse this morning. 'He's asking all the old boozers from The Plumbers' and he seems to think he can get some of the family together. So you'd better come, you and Liz. Got to keep my end up.'

'Have you told Sasha?' asked Gary.

'Not yet,' said Nick. 'I didn't know until I came back from hers last night.'

'I don't think she'll be very pleased,' said Gary cautiously. 'She and Liz have had their heads together for ages, planning something.'

'Oh, hell,' said Nick. 'All this fuss. You know what I'd like? I'd like to get on the bike and go to some place where there was nobody at all, by the sea somewhere, or up on the top of some hill, where it was dead quiet. And I'd think, there you are.

17

You've lived for twenty-one years. So what.'

'You *would* be popular,' said Gary. 'Trouble is, things like birthdays are sort of public.'

'I don't want to be public,' said Nick. 'I don't want anyone expecting anything.'

Len looked up from his ancient car-seat and said, 'Mr Towell's expecting that Escort finished by five o'clock this evening, that's all I know.'

'He'll be lucky,' said Nick.

It was ten to eight by the time the spray-job on the Escort was finished, and Mr Towell grumbled. He was a young man not much older than Nick himself, wearing a pale grey suit. He arrived in a Rover driven by a middle-aged woman.

'Frightful nuisance, having to turn out at this time of night,' he said, surveying the repaired Escort without enthusiasm. 'My mother's had to leave my father entertaining guests on his own, and I *had* planned to take my girl friend out.'

'So had I,' said Nick.

The young man ignored this. He frowned at the car. 'Did you do the brakes?' he asked.

'Nobody mentioned brakes,' said Nick.

'I distinctly told your boss they were spongy,' said Mr Towell peevishly. 'I said, I probably wouldn't have hit the blasted lamp-post if the brakes had been okay.'

'Of course you wouldn't,' his mother chimed in. 'It's really a bit much, Jeremy. These people just don't bother.'

Nick opened the Escort's door, slid into the driving seat and thumped his foot on the brake pedal several times. 'Feels well up,' he said. He released the bonnet catch, got out and checked the hydraulic fluid level. It was almost full. He glanced at the wheels, but they were dry. No sign of a caliper leaking. He closed the bonnet, pulled the dust-cover off the driving seat and wiped the wheel with it and said, 'You'll find Len in the office.'

'Just like that?' Mr Towell's mother sounded scandalised. 'You're not going to do anything about the brakes?'

'Not at this time of night, no,' said Nick. 'I've just put in two hours' overtime to get your son's car ready for him, and I'm

18

going home. If Len had thought the brakes wanted adjusting, he'd have said so.'

Len came out of the office. He had taken his overalls off and was wearing his anorak. 'All right, Mr Towell?' he asked with his professional smile.

'I don't like taking cheek from young mechanics,' said Mrs Towell before her son could answer. She glared at Nick.

'Cheek?' enquired Len warily.

'I distinctly asked for the brakes to be adjusted,' said Jeremy Towell. 'And when my mother asked if it had been done, this boy was quite rude.'

Nick looked at Len. 'You didn't say anything about the brakes,' he said. 'And I've been busting a gut to get the spray-job finished.'

Mrs Towell turned her eyes away with a pained expression and Len cleared his throat uneasily. 'Er – I did have a look at the brakes myself,' he said. 'I had the car on the rolling road this morning. But the braking distance is quite okay.'

Mr Towell looked sulky and his mother sighed. 'I told you, Jeremy, you should have taken it to a good garage,' she said. 'It's a false economy, going to these back-street places. They do this trick of leaving your car until late so they can charge double-time for the work. I wasn't born yesterday.'

Nick ripped his boiler-suit undone with an aggressive sound of parting Velcro and started to climb out of it. 'I've been working on your bloody car since eight o'clock this morning,' he said. 'Non-stop. And that's all the thanks I get.'

'Now, Nick,' Len began warningly. 'Don't be – '

'You crawl if you want to,' said Nick recklessly. 'They're your punters. I don't have to.' He bundled up the boiler-suit and slung it across the workshop to land in a sprawling heap in Len's car-seat. 'Me, I'm just the mug who does the work.' He walked off to prevent himself from saying anything more, and grabbed his jacket and crash helmet from the pegs outside the toilet. The gibe about the overtime stung. Six measly quid he'd earned in that two hours. He'd only stayed because Len said the bloke urgently needed the car for work. Work! Mr Wet Towell didn't look as if he knew what work was.

19

Buckling up his crash helmet, Nick had to walk past the Escort and the little group arguing beside it on his way out of the garage. They all stopped and looked at him. He paused and said, 'By the way, Mr Towell, what is it you work at?'

'I'm a salesman, actually,' said Jeremy, his face turning a little pink. 'I sell high-quality fitted kitchens. If it's anything to do with you.'

'Fitted kitchens!' Nick gave a snort of derisive laughter as he walked away. How mad life was, he thought as he ducked to get through the small door let into the big sliding one. Fitted bloody kitchens. In his mind's eye he saw Maurice chucking an empty beer can into the bucket under the sink in their own kitchen, and the greyish patch on the floor where the U-bend dripped. It had often infuriated and depressed him that the old man was so aggressively opposed to anything he called 'fancy', but now the fury and depression had somehow turned round. Who needed a fitted kitchen, anyway? 'Load of fancy rubbish,' he muttered to himself.

It was a relief to get on the bike and ride away from the garage, through the dusty, still-sunny streets.

'Oh, hello,' said Sasha coolly as she opened the door. 'I didn't think you were coming, not as late as this. We're just watching a film, actually.'

She turned away to the sitting-room but Nick caught her arm. 'Hang on,' he said, pushing the front door shut behind him with his boot. 'What's all this off-hand business? I can't help being late. I had to do some overtime – Len wanted a car finished. Wish I hadn't, as it happens.'

She had her chin in the air, not meeting his eye, the way she did when she was upset. 'It's all right,' she said.

Nick sagged. 'For God's sake,' he said. 'I've just come from work and I'm starving hungry. I don't know what you're fed up about, but I've had enough of stroppy people for one day.' He turned to the front door again. 'I'm off down the caff for something to eat. See you.'

'Oh, Nick, wait!' Sasha was instantly contrite. 'I'm sorry. Can I come with you?'

'Thought you were watching a film.'

Sasha shook her head and said, 'It doesn't matter.' She went to the sitting-room door and called, 'Mum, Nick and I are popping out for a bit. Won't be long.'

From the doorstep, Nick heard the tones of a pained remonstration from the sitting-room. Then Sasha came out. She ran upstairs for her crash helmet and gave it to him to hold while she struggled into her anorak. She always seemed to make such a big deal of riding the bike, he thought, waiting for her impatiently. In fact, she made a big deal of everything. Whatever she did, it always *mattered*. Still feeling irritable as she climbed on the bike behind him, he wondered why he bothered. He had never meant it to be a long-lasting affair. He had simply fancied this pink-haired girl who'd been working in a shoe shop, last summer . . . . He turned his head slightly. 'All right?' he asked.

She was fussing with her visor, but she nodded and said, 'All right.'

Nick accelerated away down the road fast and felt Sasha grab him round the waist quickly in the standard pillion-rider panic about being left sitting in the road. He grinned to himself. He would like to get Mrs Towell on the back of a bike, he thought. Just for five minutes.

The sign on Ron's Café door still said 'Open', but the chairs were standing on the tables and Ron was wiping the counter. 'Oh, Gawd,' he said as Nick and Sasha came in. 'Here comes trouble. Ain't you two got no homes to go to?'

'Oh, go on,' said Nick. 'I'm starving. And I'm sick of Chinese take-away.'

'That sauce they use looks like nail varnish,' agreed Sasha.

'Well, you'd know about that, darling,' said Ron. 'What d'you want, then? I'm not doing chips. The fryer's gone cool and I'm not hotting it up again just for two.'

'One,' corrected Sasha. 'I've eaten.'

'Even worse,' said Ron. 'Do you bacon and egg and beans if you like, Nick.'

'And a bit of fried bread,' said Nick. 'Thick bit. And we'll have two cups of tea. Please,' he added as Ron gave him a warning look.

Ron nodded, appeased, and slapped three slices of buttered bread on a plate. 'Sit over there at the shelf,' he said. 'I don't want to start cleaning tables again. I'll bring your tea in a minute.'

'Thanks,' said Sasha, and carried Nick's bread and butter across for him.

Nick wedged the crash helmets in two upturned chairs and perched on a stool. Through a mouthful of bread, he asked, 'What were you so huffy about when I came?'

Sasha looked defensive. 'Liz rang me,' she said. 'To say all the plans were changed about your birthday. And I just thought, if you'd been meaning all along to have a party at your place, you might have said, that's all.'

'I haven't been meaning anything,' said Nick crossly. 'When I got back from yours last night, the old man came out with this stupid idea about having a party. I told Gary about it this morning, and now he's got Liz living with him he can't wait to shove off home as early as he can. So I suppose he told her, while I was still at work, and she got it all wrong as usual. And now you're giving *me* a hard time about it. You think I *want* a flaming party?'

Sasha ducked her face between her hands in shame. Then she looked up at him. 'I should have guessed it wasn't your doing,' she said. 'I really am sorry.' She smiled a little sadly. 'I never seem to get it right, do I? I never know when to trust you. I'm such a twit.'

'You make it all such hard work,' said Nick.

She looked away, hurt. Ron brought the tea and said, 'I hope you two aren't quarrelling.'

'No,' said Nick. 'Not more than usual.'

When Ron had gone away again, Sasha said, 'So what about this party? It's going to be at your flat, is it?'

Nick nodded, chewing and stirring and sipping. 'Dad says he'll give it a coat of paint,' he said.

'Perhaps you could have it at ours,' Sasha suggested cautiously. 'I mean, there'd be more space.'

'Don't be silly,' said Nick. 'Can you imagine my father and his cronies having a booze-up in your house? What on earth would your mother say?'

Sasha gave a malevolent chuckle. 'It would be good for her,' she said. 'Shock therapy. There are times when I'd really like to *do* something to my mother. Liz was going to cook a slap-up birthday meal, you see. Sunday's her day off from the restaurant, so it fitted just right. And Mum was going to help as well. She's going to throw an awful fit when she hears it's all off. She'll think she's been rejected.'

Nick could imagine. A vision of Mrs Bowman's resigned face rose before him, a hand putting back a strand of the lank, faded hair in a gesture of utter weariness.

'The worst thing is,' Sasha went on, 'my father was going to come. I talked it over with Mum, then rang him up and asked him, and Laura said she wouldn't mind. I know it might have been a bit tense, the first time he'd been back to the house, but he did say, if we were planning anything for your birthday, he'd like to be counted in.'

'You're off your head,' said Nick.

'Yes,' said Sasha cheerfully. 'Always have been. Sanity's boring. I did think it would work, though, so long as – '

'This is supposed to be some sort of celebration!' Nick interrupted. 'And what do we get? People with all kinds of heavy hang-ups dragged together for a thoroughly emotional evening. That's not a party, it's bloody group therapy.'

'Oh, for God's sake,' said Sasha. 'Everyone's trying to do something nice for you, and you complain because they've got problems of their own. People can't *help* having lives that are in a muddle. You're so *selfish*, Nick.'

'You tell 'im, love,' advised Ron, arriving with a large plateful of food. 'Here you are, Nick. Found you a couple of bangers as well.'

'Oh, great,' said Nick. 'Thanks a lot. Can I have some more bread?'

'Come and get it,' said Ron.

Returning, Nick said through a mouthful, 'That's the way people ought to be. Like Ron. Do whatever it is they do, and give you a decent deal if they can.'

'And that's all?' asked Sasha.

'It's enough,' said Nick.

Sasha watched him while he ate. When he had finished, she said flatly, 'I can't face telling Mum.'

Nick profoundly wished that the next couple of weeks could simply not happen. He wondered if he could ask for another cup of tea, but Ron was leaning against the cash register, reading the paper in an attitude of ostentatious waiting, and he decided that he'd better not. Sasha was frowning at him. He sighed. 'You'd better ask her to this do of Dad's, then,' he said. It was a fair bet she wouldn't come. 'And your father, too. Ask anyone you like.'

Sasha's face did not brighten. 'I suppose it's the best we can do,' she said. 'Dad will probably be all right – but I think Mum might feel she's intruding.'

Good, Nick thought. Sasha looked at him suspiciously and he said, 'Tell her it's an exercise in sociology. See how the other half lives. She won't be able to refuse then, in case we think she's a snob. Which she is.'

Sasha laughed, appalled and guilty. She put her hand over Nick's and said, 'I don't know why I love you. You're the most awful person I know.'

'I'm the *only* awful person you know,' said Nick.

Ron put his paper down and said, 'All right, you two. You've had your nosh. You can do your murmuring sweet nothings in some other place. One-forty, please, Nick.'

Nick fished out two pound coins and gave them to Ron with a vague flap of his hand to indicate that he didn't want any change. 'One day you can give me a cup of tea when I'm broke,' he said.

'What about all the ones you've had?' demanded Ron. 'Go on – shove off.'

'Okay,' said Nick peaceably.

Ron shook his head as he opened the door to let them out and turned the hanging notice to read CLOSED. 'Don't know what you see in him, love,' he said to Sasha. 'Nice girl like you.'

She smiled at him radiantly. 'Neither do I,' she said. And

24

Nick remembered all over again why it was that he had fancied the pink-haired girl in the shoe shop.

Still missing his second cup of tea, Nick headed for the pub on the corner, ignoring Sasha's half-hearted protests about having to be up early the next morning. Three lagers later, he felt warm and relaxed and deeply disinclined to move. A pleasant ache spread through his limbs like a generalised echo of the day's discomforts and he sat slumped in the corner of a buttoned leather seat with his eyes half-shut.

'Anyone would think you'd been working,' said Sasha teasingly.

Nick did not answer. The fact that he was not at this moment crouching beside a car, with the details of its surface large before his eyes, was enough. Conversation could not add to the contentment. But Sasha's comment triggered off a mental replay of the day's long, repetitive, muscle-wearying work, and he frowned, not wanting to think about it.

'Sorry I spoke,' said Sasha, piqued. 'You ought to have a sign on you like a loo door, saying Occupied. Then I wouldn't bang on it.'

The barman draped a towel over the beer handles and Nick reluctantly pulled himself together. 'Yes, you would,' he said. 'You'd count up to about ten, then you'd start shouting, "Come on, hurry up." I know you.'

'I don't think you know me at all,' said Sasha. 'You're not interested in what I'm really like. As long as I look okay and fit in with your life, you don't want to know anything else.'

'Charming,' said Nick. 'On that basis, I might be sitting here with any old slag.'

'Yes,' said Sasha without amusement. 'I think you might.'

Nick reached up an arm and put it round her shoulders lazily. It was quite some time since they had spent the night together. That's why she was so fretful. 'Will your mum have gone to bed by now?' he asked.

'Probably,' said Sasha. 'But it doesn't matter if she hasn't, does it?' She slipped her hand inside his open leather jacket and he felt it creep up his shirt like a small, urgent animal. He had an insane desire to set about her there and then on the bottle-

25

green smoothness of the leather-upholstered pub seat.

'Time, sir, please,' said the barman, knocking out the ashtray into a bucket and giving the table a rapid wipe with a cloth.

Nick pushed his tobacco tin into his pocket and stood up, holding Sasha's hand. 'Come on,' he said. 'Time to go home.'

Chapter 3

On his way to work the next morning, Nick pulled up at red traffic lights, reflecting with some satisfaction on his success in avoiding Mrs Bowman. The wretched woman insisted on getting up in the morning to cut sandwiches for Sasha, so Nick had escaped to Ron's for an early breakfast. There had been some witty comments from Ron, but anything was better than the puffy-faced silence and that awful droopy dressing gown. Its faded paeonies were so like their owner's face.

Nick grinned at the thought and pushed up his visor for a clearer look at the world. These were three-way traffic lights and the wait was always a long one.

'*Nick*!' shouted a girl's voice from the sports car beside him. 'You old stinker! How are you?'

Nick looked down at her and recognised Claudia, an ex-girl friend. 'Hello, Claud,' he said. 'Like the new car. Present from Daddy?'

'Yes, for my twenty-first,' said Claudia. 'You still unemployed?'

'No, I'm a garage mechanic, aren't I?' said Nick. 'What you doing out of bed so early?'

'I'm a working girl these days,' said Claudia with her goofy smile. 'Apprentice hairdresser.'

'That's not work,' said Nick. 'It's just one of your amusements.' A Fiat X 19 for your birthday, he thought — you don't have to work. 'Here,' he said on impulse, 'it's *my* twenty-first Sunday week. You want to come? Bring whoever your man is now.' That'll be a shock to the system of some upper-class twit, he thought. It was a kind of one-in-the-eye for Jeremy Towell.

'I will,' said Claudia. Then, as the lights changed, 'See you.'

Nick heard the Fiat's engine rev, but he was quicker, and grinned as he heard the squeal of tyre-slip from behind him, with a honk from a taxi's horn. Old Claud had never mastered the racing get-away. But, even with the triumphant reflection, an uneasiness stirred within him. Why on earth had he invited her to the party? Sasha would be furious. He slipped through the narrow gap between two buses and mentally shrugged. The party was going to be terrible in any case. Sexpot Claud and some Hooray Henry couldn't make it any worse.

Len came out of the office and said, 'Want a word with you, Nick.'

'Oh, yes?' said Nick. He followed Len back into the tiny room with its one-bar electric fire and its stacks of box files.

'Just watch it,' Len told him. 'I can't afford to lose customers because of your big mouth. Those people last night – it's not the first time I've had complaints about you being rude. Look at that chap with the Mercedes. You called him a prat and he takes the car to Palmers now.'

'But he was going on about the carburettor, and the bloody thing's a diesel,' said Nick.

'I know it's a diesel,' said Len. 'And I know he's a prat. But he was an expensive prat, and I've lost him, and it's your fault. What I'm saying to you is, just keep your mouth shut in future. I've told you before, and I'm telling you again. I don't want any more cheek like you handed out to the Towells last night.'

'But you didn't ask me to look at his blasted brakes!' protested Nick. 'What was I supposed to do?'

'If a punter complains, refer him to me,' said Len, tapping himself on the chest. 'Politely.' His eyes, Nick thought, were the colour of cold tea. 'And don't try and be clever. If there's one thing I can't stand, it's clever bastards.'

'Don't worry,' said Nick. 'I only got two "O" Levels.'

Len was not reassured. 'You could have got more if you tried,' he said darkly. 'I know your sort. Now, shove off.'

Nick was not quite sure if he was still employed, but Len shouted after him, 'Mrs Beale's Morris Minor wants a plate welded underneath. Jim'll show you.'

'Right,' said Nick.

At half-past twelve Gary appeared beside the deeply unhealthy Morris Minor and said, 'Coming down the park? I hate staying in here when it's sunny.'

'Yeah, okay,' said Nick, getting up. 'I was going down the sandwich bar anyway, to get something.'

Gary picked up his lunch box and they set out. 'Oversleep, did you?' he asked. 'No time to make your sarnies?'

'Can't make sarnies in Mrs Bowman's kitchen,' said Nick.

'Ah,' said Gary. 'No, you wouldn't. Is she still miserable?'

'*Is* she,' said Nick with feeling. 'I think she enjoys it. She hates anyone trying to cheer her up. Gets really stroppy.'

'I suppose being alone is still new to her,' said Gary. 'Liz's mum has always been on her own, give or take the occasional boy-friend. But she's a tough old bird.'

'Yes,' agreed Nick. He thought about Liz's mother, scrawny-armed and with one eye shut against the smoke from her perpetual cigarette. 'But then, she's a different sort.'

'Yeah,' said Gary. He waited outside the shop while Nick went in and bought two cheese rolls and a can of Coke, then they set off again. Abruptly, he asked, 'Is Sasha on the pill?'

'Course she's on the pill,' said Nick. 'She didn't really like the idea but I wasn't taking that sort of risk. I mean, what d'you think I am, suicidal or something?'

'Speaking as a dead man,' said Gary, 'I wouldn't know.' He glanced at Nick's startled face and said, 'That's right. I'm going to be a dad. Liz is pregnant.'

'Oh, heck,' said Nick. He felt horrified, and faintly smug. It was to prevent exactly this disaster that he had gone along with Sasha to cheer her up in the Family Planning clinic with its flowered curtains and its kindly-smiling ladies. He had bought a huge bunch of grapes from the stall at the hospital gate and handed them round to everyone so they were all giggling as to what to do with the pips. But it was Liz herself who told Sasha about the clinic, when she'd been objecting that her family doctor had pudgy little hands and steamed-up glasses. And now – Liz, of all people! What on earth had gone wrong? He gazed at Gary in concern. 'What are you going to do?' he asked.

Gary shrugged. 'It's not up to me,' he said. 'Liz did it on purpose. She says she'd been thinking about having a baby for ages, and decided she would. I can stick around and be its father if I want to, she says. If not, not.'

Nick looked at his friend, astonished by his lack of outrage. 'And do you want to?' he asked.

'May as well,' said Gary, but his attempted nonchalance was cracked by a delighted smile. 'She's quite a girl, is Liz,' he added, trying to disguise it as admiration.

'You old bugger, you're like a dog with two tails,' said Nick. 'Hit the jackpot, haven't you. Are you going to get married?' It seemed incredible. Marriage – children – all that belonged to an older generation. Surely he and Gary hadn't arrived there yet?

'Liz doesn't much want to,' Gary admitted. 'She's quite prepared to go it alone. Sort of not wanting to rely on anyone else, I suppose. But I mean, it's my baby too. And I've been working at Len's ever since I left school, so I've got a bit put by. I'd been thinking of trying to get a place of my own, anyway. So I think it would be best if we got married and found a place together.'

Nick laughed. 'Things could have been worse,' he said. 'At least you can make up your own mind about it. Better than having some heavy father on the doorstep with a shotgun.'

'Liz hasn't got a father, thank God,' said Gary. Then he realised the significance of this remark, and clapped a hand to his head. 'Just think, her kid's father is going to be *me*. What's that kid going to think I'm like? If he's walking along some pavement like we are now, in twenty-one years' time, when he's our age, what'll he be saying about me? He or she,' he added, looking even more anxious.

'Don't worry,' said Nick drily. 'In twenty-one years there may not be any pavements. Or any kids or fathers or any world at all.'

They turned in through the park gates and started to walk

29

across the dry, rubbish-littered grass.

'You've got to assume there will be, though,' Gary objected. 'Otherwise, what's the point of anything?'

'Not a lot,' said Nick. 'I used to think about it when we were at school. Old Green would be carrying on because I wasn't wearing a tie or something fatuous, and I'd just imagine us all vaporised. Whoof! Ties and all. It was great.'

'But you can't live like that,' said Gary, sitting down on a bench and pulling the lid off his lunch box. 'If we knew the big bang was coming next week, it would be different. But we don't.'

Nick fished a cheese roll out of his paper bag. 'How would it be different?' he asked. 'What would you do in that last week that you don't do now?'

'I wouldn't go to work,' said Gary promptly. 'I'd scrape up all the money I could, and take Liz somewhere nice. By the sea, perhaps. We'd have a really good time.'

'We all ought to have a good time all the time,' said Nick indistinctly, through a mouthful.

'Don't be stupid,' said Gary. 'Good times cost money.'

The sky above the yellowing plane trees was a hazy, dusty blue. Nick leaned back, chewing, and stared at it. 'Things are all wrong, somehow,' he said. 'I think everything could be good. *Is* good, in a way. People muck it up, that's all.'

'You do talk a load of rubbish,' said Gary.

''Spect so,' agreed Nick amiably. It was never any use trying to explain how he felt. People never understood. He wished he understood it better himself. He had never made any conscious decision to take a different view of life from other people; it was just that 'normality', as they called it at school, had seemed more and more weird. It was such a lousy bargain, years and years and years of monotonous work given in exchange for just enough money so you didn't have to turn up at the DHSS every week. Even if you earned quite a lot, what did it buy? A bigger house, a better car, a video, an extra week of holiday in the working year. It wasn't good enough. Time was precious. 'I got a bawling-out from Len this morning,' he said. 'Thought he was going to sack me.' He found that he regarded this possibility with a tinge of regret. He had been at Bennett's Garage for nearly a year now. A hell of a long time.

'You want to watch it,' said Gary. 'With Palmers poshing up their forecourt and doing all that advertising, we've lost a lot of customers lately. Len wouldn't be sorry to cut down a bit. D'you want this custard tart? I don't like them much, and Mum will put them in.'

'Slurpy, aren't they,' said Nick, accepting it. He never turned down the offer of food.

'Roll on Monday week,' said Gary, yawning and stretching his skinny arms above his head. 'A whole fortnight of freedom.'

'You'll come back knackered,' said Nick. 'All those Swedish birds.'

'Some chance,' retorted Gary. 'Liz is coming too, don't forget.'

'Your pregnant fiancée,' said Nick mockingly. 'You staying with those people your sister works for again?'

'Yes,' said Gary. 'They've got this socking great house beside a lake, only about an hour's drive from Stockholm. They're very nice to Jenny. Let her use the car and everything.'

'Seems a bit back to front,' said Nick. 'You always hear about Swedish *au pairs* over here, but not the other way round.'

'It's to help the kids practise their English,' Gary explained. 'They take it really seriously.'

'Money for jam,' said Nick. 'And if you don't like it, you can always drop the kids in the lake and shove off somewhere else.'

Gary laughed. 'Sounds right up your street,' he said. 'Nick the nanny.'

'No,' said Nick with regret. 'I'm not house-trained.'

'You're not even garage-trained,' said Gary. He glanced at his watch and said, 'We've got ten minutes yet. Good.' And, turning his face to the hazy sun, he folded his arms and closed his eyes.

Pipe and slippers for you, mate, Nick said to him silently, and felt a kind of sadness. Gary had moved away as certainly as if he had stepped on to a conveyor-belt. In his mind's eye, Nick could see his retreating, middle-aged back. He opened his can of

31

Coke and threw the ring-pull at his dozing friend. It hit him on the nose, but Gary merely smiled tolerantly and did not open his eyes.

'Sorry, Dad,' said Nick.

After work, Nick headed towards Croydon. The idea of going to see his mother had stayed in his mind, and the chance meeting with Claudia had somehow reinforced it. His mother had liked Claudia, in a contemptuous sort of way. 'She's like one of those stupid rabbits with long fur,' she had said. 'Stick it in a field and it wouldn't know how to eat grass, but it's pretty. Same with her. Useless, but she's got style.' Nick remembered Claudia's toothy grin and the long blonde hair which fell across one eye. She would raise a lazy scarlet-nailed finger to push it back and dart a seductive glance at Nick. 'Such a *rough* boy,' she would say. No, his mother was wrong about Claud. She was far better armed than a rabbit. More like a mink.

The pub in Croydon was a hideous one, brown-tiled to shoulder height, on the corner of a busy road junction. The fence which ran along the side road from its rear had a notice on its gate which said 'To The Garden'. Nick nudged the gate open with the front wheel of his bike and rode in, narrowly missing a tall, balding man carrying a crate of bottles.

'You can't bring that in here,' said the man, then, as Nick killed the engine and took off his crash helmet, 'Oh, it's you.'

'That's what I like about you, Tim,' said Nick, heaving the bike on to its stand. 'Always a cheery welcome. Is Mum around?'

'She's in the bar,' said Tim. 'Look, just put the bike over there, will you? By the dustbins. The customers won't like it on the lawn.'

'Okay,' said Nick. Personally, he felt that the bike was a much less offensive object than most of Tim's customers, from what he had seen of them, but he wasn't going to argue. He moved it, then went in through the kitchen door.

'Barbie!' he heard Tim call. 'Nick's here.'

His mother came in from the bar. She was barely shoulder-high to Nick, with the unruly mass of dark hair which he had inherited, and she looked professionally sexy in her red trousers and frilly blouse. 'Nicky!' she said. 'How are you?' She was the only person who ever called him Nicky. She hugged him, then stood with her hands on his shoulders, smiling up at him. Her eyes were the same clear blue as his own, but the skin round them was wrinkled under its pancake make-up, and the spiky lashes were blobby with carelessly-applied mascara.

'Fine,' said Nick. 'You look great. How are things?'

'Oh, can't grumble,' said Barbie. 'What about you? How's your dad?'

'He *can* grumble,' said Nick. 'And does.'

'Old git,' said Barbie automatically. 'So what are you up to? Still at the garage? Here, do you want a drink? On the house.'

'Tea,' said Nick. 'Yeah, still at Len's.'

'You must like it,' said his mother. 'That's a long time for you to be in one place.' She dropped teabags into two mugs and switched on the kettle. 'What about Sasha? Still seeing her?'

'Yeah, still seeing her,' said Nick. And that was it, really, he thought. All news exchanged. Purpose of visit over. What a bloody dull life, if it could be summed up like that, in about two minutes.

'Your dad rang me up last week,' said Barbie. 'First time in years — gave me quite a turn. I thought there'd been an accident. But it was about your twenty-first. Seems you're having a party.'

'*He's* having a party,' Nick corrected. 'I don't want anything to do with it.'

'Be a laugh if you don't turn up,' said his mother. 'Can you imagine? Talk about do his nut.'

'Perhaps I could come and see you instead,' said Nick, seizing a faint hope. 'You wouldn't let on, would you?'

Barbie looked guilty. 'Matter of fact, he's a jump ahead of you,' she said. 'He's asked me to do the catering.'

'Oh, no!' Nick put a hand over his eyes, then took it away again. 'And you're going to?'

'I said I would, yes,' agreed Barbie. 'I couldn't refuse, really, the way he put it. I mean, he'd got a point. If we'd still been together, I'd have done all sorts of things for you, over the years. As it is — well, helping out with your twenty-first is the least I can do.'

Nick blew a long sigh. This was getting worse.

'He caught me on the hop, really,' Barbie admitted. 'I should have known it wasn't your sort of thing. But the way he talked about it, I thought it was all fixed.'

'Oh, it's fixed all right,' said Nick. 'But he didn't choose to mention it to me, that's all. Not until two nights ago.'

Tim put his head round the door and said, 'There's a hell of a lot of people in the lounge, Barbie.'

'Okay,' said Barbie. 'Be out in a second. D'you want something to eat, Nicky?' she added. 'We've got pies and pasties hot, and I can do some beans.'

'Great,' said Nick. 'Then I'll give you a hand serving in the bar if you're busy.'

His mother looked at him. 'You don't have to pay for your meals, love,' she said. 'Not here.'

'It isn't like that,' Nick said quickly. 'I wouldn't mind helping, that's all.'

But he knew it was like that. He understood how Liz felt about her baby. Not wanting to be beholden to anyone. As though, if the world did come to an end, there would be no unfinished business. No debts.

Chapter 4

The smell of paint hit him as he opened the door of the flat. He went into the sitting-room and stared round. 'Christ,' he said.

The room was coated with a violent yellowish green, the colour, Nick thought, of rotting cabbages. Maurice stood on a chair, completing the last corner by the window. He turned, pot in hand, and said, 'Like it?'

'Cabbages,' said Nick faintly. 'Slime.'

'It's lime green, yeah,' agreed his father, looking at the label

34

on the tin. 'Told you I'd do the place up.'

Nick permitted himself a brief dream of pushing Maurice, complete with brush and pot of terrible paint, out of the window. He watched him gyrate his way down past the twelve floors, followed by a spiral of Slime Green, to land — he blinked. 'For God's sake,' he said. 'Why green? Why *that* green?'

'It was some Terry had by him,' Maurice admitted. 'Two quid the lot. I mean, can't look a gift horse in the mouth, boy.'

'I would if the bloody thing was going to bite me,' said Nick. He stared round the room in disbelief. 'It isn't undercoat, is it?' he asked.

'No, I put the first coat on last night,' said Maurice. 'When you was tucked up with some bird, I suppose, since you didn't choose to come home. This is it. Done. And I got some cream for the woodwork.'

Nick almost said that paint would be better, but decided against it.

Maurice filled in the last corner while Nick watched helplessly, then got down from his chair. He put the tin on a newspaper on the floor, retrieved its lid from the windowsill, fitted it on and trod it home with his foot. Then he carried the brush into the kitchen, and Nick heard the tap running. He sat down on the arm of the sofa and tried not to look at the hideous walls. It was difficult. They loomed in on him oppressively. *Everything* seemed to be looming in. Nick could not quite put his finger on what was causing a sense of dread — apart from the green walls and the party — but it was there, all the same, a feeling that some sort of doom was catching up with him. A whole year in the same job, and with the same girl friend. Len's ultimatum, Gary's defection to the ranks of the respectable. They were ominous portents.

Maurice came back, wiping his hands on the kitchen towel, and said, 'You don't like it, do you?'

Nick knew he had to lie. 'It'll be all right,' he said. 'Just takes a bit of getting used to. It's — unusual.'

'That's what I thought,' agreed Maurice. 'He's got an eye for a colour, has Terry.'

'Which one?' asked Nick unkindly. All he could remember

about Terry was his squint.

When Nick went round to Sasha's house the next evening, he did not for a moment recognise the woman who opened the door. Her hair was a uniform beige colour, bouffed into a meringue above the ears, with a curly fringe which made its owner look, he thought, like a superannuated Julie Andrews.

Joanna Bowman blushed slightly under his scrutiny and said, 'Do you like it? I had it done yesterday.' She touched her unfamiliar hair tentatively, as though it might crumble or melt.

'Smashing,' said Nick bravely.

'Susan rang to say she'd be late home,' said Joanna, standing back to let Nick in. 'It seems the Abrahams have got some sort of rush job on. I don't expect she'll be long now. Would you like a sherry?'

Nick had not stopped for anything to eat and he was very hungry, but somehow he found himself in Mrs Bowman's sitting-room, cursing himself for not being firmer.

'Sweet or dry?' asked Joanna.

'Dry, please,' said Nick. In fact he did not like dry sherry very much, but to choose it implied, he thought, that he was being correct and not too familiar. Mrs Bowman always made him feel cautious when she was being amiable. With a friend, it would be different. He thought of Claudia, who used to like brightly-coloured drinks with cherries and ice and stripey straws.

'I really prefer sweet,' said Joanna. She brought the drinks on a lacquered Chinese tray, with a bowl of peanuts. 'Well — cheers,' She seemed to have adopted a bolder manner with her new hairstyle.

'Cheers,' said Nick, helping himself to the nuts. He wished he had admitted to preferring sweet.

After a pause, Joanna said, 'It was so nice of you and Sasha — as you call her — to ask me to your party. That's why I had my hair done. I thought I really should make an effort. The girl said it'll need a week or so to settle down, then I can have a shampoo and set just before the day.'

'Er — what did Sasha say about the party, then?' Nick
36

enquired, appalled by this rapid turn of events.

'She explained that your father hadn't known we had plans for you of our own,' said Joanna. 'So he'd sent out all the invitations and booked the caterers and everything. Well, I couldn't expect him to cancel such a big commitment. I can't pretend I wasn't disappointed.' She smiled bravely. 'It's not as if I have much to look forward to these days. But Sasha said you and she both felt the day wouldn't be complete if I wasn't there.'

Nick gulped. 'And is Sasha's dad coming, too?' he asked.

'I know David has been approached,' said Joanna stiffly. She stared down at her sherry glass and added, 'I shall find it very difficult. Susan says it will be a good thing to meet on neutral ground, rather than here, with all its memories.' She glanced round the room as if reproaching the furniture for its tacit part in the upheaval.

The front door banged and Sasha came in, wearing a long white cardigan over a short yellow frock. She looked tired. 'I didn't know you were coming round, or I'd have rung you at work to say I'd be late,' she said to Nick.

'It's all right. Better not to ring the garage, anyway,' Nick said. 'Len doesn't like personal calls to the staff.'

'Telling me,' said Sasha. 'Last time I rang, he said what did I think he was, your bloody secretary.' But Nick knew her mind was not on what she was saying. 'Don't you think Mum's hair looks nice?' she added coaxingly.

'It's great,' said Nick. 'I already said.' He met Sasha's eye reprovingly. He'd agreed that her mother would have to be asked, but there'd been no need to twist her arm about it. He scooped up the last of the peanuts.

'Have you eaten?' Sasha asked him.

'No,' said Nick. 'Except for the peanuts. Sorry. I've been a bit of a hog.'

'They were there to be eaten,' said Joanna magnanimously. 'There's cauliflower cheese keeping hot in the oven, Su — er, Sasha.' She glanced at Nick dubiously and added, 'I suppose it might run to three.'

'No problem,' said Nick, draining his glass. 'I'll go round to the caff. I'm not too keen on cauliflower cheese anyway.' He

37

stood up and added to Sasha, 'We can talk another time.'

'Don't go,' pleaded Sasha. 'I mean – I won't be long.'

'If you want to go and eat in some greasy café, that's all right,' said her mother, tight-lipped. 'But I wouldn't have bothered cooking if I'd known. A sandwich is enough for me.'

'Here we go again,' said Nick, abandoning all politeness with a sense of relief. He picked up his crash helmet and added, 'I'll be in Ron's. For a bit, anyway. Come down later if you feel like it. Thanks for the sherry, Mrs Bowman. And the nuts.'

'But it's twenty minutes' walk,' protested Sasha. 'And if I come down there and you've gone, where will you be?'

Nick frowned. '*I* don't know,' he said impatiently, and went. As he closed the door, he heard their voices raised in argument.

Sasha ought to get herself a bike, he thought as he straddled the Kawa and started its engine. A little 125 would do her perfectly well. He rode off, thinking about it. Being without transport was a blasted nuisance. Look at tonight. By the time she'd eaten the dreaded cauliflower cheese and had a cup of coffee and talked her mother out of her sulks, it would be getting on for eight o'clock, and then there'd be twenty minutes' walk on top of that. She couldn't expect him to wait for nearly two hours. And anyway, he hadn't said where he'd be afterwards, so probably she wouldn't bother.

Relieved of the need to think any further about the vague and unsatisfactory arrangements, Nick pulled up outside an orange-lit Pizzeria. He was bored with Ron's greasy-spoon food, anyway, and this place was just as cheap.

He was finishing a large plate of spaghetti when a lad detached himself from a group sitting at a table across the aisle and slid into the vacant chair opposite Nick. 'You're Nick Cartwright, aren't you?' he asked.

Nick raised his eyebrows and mopped up some sauce with a bit of bread.

'Sorry bothering you,' said the boy. 'My name's Stevie Brent. I remember you from school – I was in the second form when you left.'

'You got a brother called Paul?' asked Nick, vaguely remembering a red-haired boy a bit older than himself.

Stevie nodded eagerly. 'That's right. Only I wondered if I could ask you about my bike. We live near Gary Weston, and I asked him, but he said you were the bloke that knew all about bikes.'

'What you got, then?' asked Nick.

'It's a C 50,' said the boy. 'Only it's making this rattling noise.'

The waitress took Nick's plate and said, 'You want something else?'

'No, thanks,' said Nick.

'Coffee?' suggested Stevie.

'Could do.'

'Two coffees,' said the waitress, and shuffled flat-footed back to the counter.

'Probably the cam chain,' said Nick. 'Where's the bike now?'

'Outside,' said Stevie. 'We could look at it at my place. There's a yard out the back.'

'Okay,' said Nick.

The rest of the evening passed pleasantly. Nick dropped in at Gary's house to borrow his socket-set, then went round to the Brents' place, which turned out to be a tall Victorian house with an open yard behind it, flanked by an odd-looking warehouse-like building. 'It used to be a mortuary,' Stevie explained. 'Where they kept the corpses before they were buried. This was an undertaker's place.'

'Charming,' said Nick.

He adjusted the C 50's cam chain and reset the timing, watched admiringly by Stevie and his awe-struck parents, neither of whom seemed capable of managing anything more complex than an alarm clock. Stevie's father was an architect, and Nick felt surprised that such a vague-seeming man could do anything as practical as designing a building.

'You ought to set up in business,' said Mr Brent as he pressed a fiver gratefully into Nick's hand. 'The bike shops round here are terrible. They charge you the earth and they seem to cause more trouble than they cure. It's my belief they put something wrong on purpose, to make sure the trade keeps coming in.'

Nick smiled non-committally and said, 'Me, set up in business? Chance would be a fine thing.' The superstitions of owners about their vehicles were beyond belief. Only last week a woman, who had brought her car in for a respray, was blaming Len the next day when her dynamo packed up. But there was no point in arguing.

He called round at Gary's house again to return his tools and this time it was Liz who opened the door. Somehow, Nick expected her to have a stomach the size of a football, but she looked the same as usual, thin as a rake, with pale ginger hair and pale eyelashes. 'Oh, hello,' she said. 'I just got in.'

'Busy night at the caff?' asked Nick.

'Restaurant,' Liz corrected. 'Mr Mandel would have a fit if he heard you call it a caff. Yes, pretty busy.'

The front door opened straight into the sitting-room and Gary's mother shouted from in front of the television, 'Sit down, Nick, you're making the place untidy. Gary's gone out for some beer,' she added, 'before they close.'

'I brought his tools back,' said Nick.

'Oh, ta,' said Mrs Weston. 'Liz, put the kettle on, love. I don't want beer, this time of night. Does things to my waterworks.'

'I've gone off it,' said Liz. 'Can't stand the smell.'

'I was like that about fags,' said Mrs Weston, flicking ash. 'Couldn't bear one anywhere near me, right up to when Gary was born. But he no sooner gave his first yell than I was trying to cadge a cigarette off the nurses.'

'It's your body telling you what it wants,' said Liz. 'Can't argue.' And she went into the kitchen.

Nick felt oddly left behind. Liz, who used to streak her hair with vermilion and stick sequins on her eyebrows, had moved away into the hierarchy of child-bearing women, able to talk about these womb-based experiences with all the aplomb of age-old knowledge. She and Mrs Weston were like a couple of benign witches. He was glad when Gary came in with the beer.

'That bird of yours rang up,' said Maurice as Nick came into the sitting-room. The green walls looked even worse now that the furniture was back in place, Nick thought. As if they were living in an aquarium with scummy glass. 'Sasha?' he queried.

'Yeah,' said Maurice. 'Think so. Seemed a bit narked.' On the television, a man in a sweat shirt with Feed The World on it was talking about God.

'What did she say?' asked Nick.

'*I* dunno,' said Maurice irritably. 'Silly cow rang in the middle of the snooker.'

'It would be the middle of something whenever she rang,' said Nick. 'I mean, look at you now. Gawping at Mr Godburger. You're not interested in all that stuff.'

'I might be,' said Maurice with his chin in the air.

Nick slumped down on the sofa. He knew what the phone call would be about. He could almost hear Sasha's voice. 'I went all the way down to Ron's,' she would say, 'and he said you hadn't even been there.' True. He hadn't. He stretched clenched fists above his head with a faint churning in his stomach like sitting in a dentist's waiting room.

The telephone rang.

'She ain't giving up easy,' said Maurice with a malicious grin. 'Go on. Face the music.'

Nick picked up the receiver and said, 'Hello.'

'You're back,' said Sasha.

'That's right,' agreed Nick.

'I went all the way down to Ron's,' she said. 'And you hadn't even been there. I waited until half-past nine. You just don't care, do you? You really are —'

Partly to keep face in front of his father and partly because of the continued churning sensation, Nick yawned, holding the receiver in the air away from him. The voice went on coming out, but its angry twitter was drowned by the closing rock-gospel music from the television.

'Women,' said Maurice. 'Who needs 'em?'

Nick looked at him. That's not what you said when Barbie walked out, he thought, remembering the anguished outbursts of self-pity and recrimination. But then, the stupid old bugger had deserved it. He turned away from Maurice's mocking grin, and brought the receiver back to his ear.

'Done it again, haven't I?' Nick said.

'You sure have,' said Sasha. And she was not laughing.

Chapter 5

The next day was a Saturday. Nick and Gary were sent out with the break-down truck to tow in a Marina with a broken clutch, and the rest of the morning went in repairing it for the agitated owner, who was fretting about meeting his wife at the East Midlands airport that afternoon.

'Whew!' said Nick as the man rushed across to the office to write a cheque for Len. 'Who'd be married? Nothing but hassle.'

'It doesn't have to be,' said Gary, then added, 'what are you doing this weekend?'

'Got to clean the bike,' said Nick. He thought of last night's telephone conversation, which had gone on long and acrimoniously after Maurice had retired, grinning, to bed. 'I said I'd take Sasha to Kew Gardens,' he said. 'She's got to do drawings of leaves and things. Something to do with her Day Release course. Fabric Design.' In fact, Sasha had said that's where she was going, and he could come or not, as he chose. She didn't care, she said.

'Liz might like that,' said Gary. 'Are you going on Sunday? We could come with you.'

Nick shook his head. 'Sasha's got a photo session on Sunday,' he said. 'Modelling new fashions for the firm's mail order catalogue. So it's got to be this afternoon.'

'We'll have to skip it, then,' said Gary. 'Liz is on split shift, doing lunch and dinner. I think she works too hard. I'd like to see her pack it in.'

The owner of the Marina came back, tucking his cheque book into his inside pocket, and Nick snatched the car's door open with a smart salute. 'All ready for you, sir,' he said.

'Thanks very much,' said the man. He got into the car and started its engine, then said, 'Here – buy yourself a drink.'

'Two quid,' said Nick, looking at what he had been given as the man drove out. 'There you go. We'll split it.'

'Ta,' said Gary, pocketing the coin. 'I don't know how you do it. Half the time you're insulting the punters, and yet you always manage to get tipped.'

'Silent menace,' said Nick. 'They tip because they want to be on the right side of you. If you're a groveller, they don't have to bother. I didn't get anything out of the Towells, though.'

'Are you surprised?' said Gary.

Sasha opened her vermilion-spotted attaché case in the narrow gangway of a particularly steamy house where huge plants dangled lengths of themselves from the glass roof in hairy profusion. She produced a sketch-book and pencil, closed the case and wedged it between her feet, and began to draw. Water dripped between the plants and the heat was stifling.

'Are you going to be long?' asked Nick.

'Possibly,' said Sasha crisply.

He sat down on the cast-iron edging of the raised bed and considered the situation. She was giving him a hard time because of last night, but if he objected, she would say she was simply drawing a plant. And she had come prepared for the tropical conditions, in brief white shorts and an off-the-shoulder cotton top. He, in jeans and a denim shirt, was sweating copiously. He undid his trainers and kicked them off and removed his socks, then stood up and pulled his shirt over his head. Then he unzipped his jeans and, hopping on first one foot and then the other, took them off as well. A crimson-faced man in a tweed suit glanced at him, scandalised, and said, 'Good God.'

'It's all right,' Nick assured him. 'I'll keep my pants on.' And he began to paddle about in the warm water which lay in pools on the grey-tiled floor. It felt very pleasant.

Sasha ignored him completely and continued to draw. Most of the other people in the house pretended not to notice Nick's near-nudity, but a party of Italians laughed a lot and a Welsh lady said, 'There's disgusting,' and hustled her staring daughter past, quickly. Then a pair of American tourists approached Nick, guide books in hand. The man, in flowered shirt and sunglasses, seemed to think Nick was stripped down for work. He said, 'Hi. Would you be the keeper around here?'

'No,' said Nick. 'I'm the inmate.' and he gibbered.

'Oh, my *Gahd*,' said the female tourist. 'For Pete's sakes, come on.' They fled.

Sasha stopped drawing and began to laugh. 'You *idiot*,' she said. 'Why on earth do I go out with you?'

'You don't have to,' Nick observed.

Sasha dumped her sketch-book on a plant which looked like a heap of dead toads and flung her arms round his neck. 'I do love you,' she said, kissing him. 'I wouldn't have anyone else, really.'

Nick enfolded her, kissing her sweaty face. In the steamy heat, they felt as slippery together as a couple of newts. Delicious, he thought. Unexpectedly, the afternoon was turning out to be very enjoyable.

At Nick's elbow, somebody gave a discreet cough and said, 'Excuse me, sir.'

Nick looked round.

'I'd be grateful if you'd put your clothes on, sir,' said the keeper, his face red with embarrassment and steam. 'Some of the visitors are complaining.'

Nick smiled. It would be more fun if they took theirs off as well, he thought. It could be quite a party. But he disengaged himself from Sasha and said mildly, 'Okay.' He gathered up his clothes and shoes and said, 'I'll get dressed outside. Too hot in here.' Officials, as he had learned at school, would put up with quite a lot of cranky behaviour as long as they were sure you were stupid.

Sasha was at his heels as he left the house. Outside, a small crowd gathered and watched him suspiciously as he put on his clothes. 'Funny,' he said to the keeper who stood supervising him, 'people mostly like to watch someone *un*dress, don't they? D'you think they'd pay? Ten p, anyone?' he asked the onlookers. 'This young lady will bring round the hat.'

'Or the sock,' said Sasha helpfully.

Muttering, the crowd began to disperse.

'Nuts, you are,' said the keeper, and he, too, moved off.

'Let's go and have a cup of tea,' said Sasha. 'There's a place over there.'

Sitting at a plastic table under the trees, Nick felt much more cheerful. He stirred his tea untidily and said, 'Are you still cross?'

'No,' said Sasha, but with a faint sigh.

'Don't sigh,' said Nick. 'It makes you seem like your mother. I don't want you to be like her.'

'I can only be whatever it is I am,' said Sasha.

Nick thought about this. 'But you can be whatever you want to be,' he objected. 'You're in charge of yourself. So if you sigh, it's because you *decide* to sigh.'

'Yes,' agreed Sasha. 'But the point is, if I decided *not* to sigh, it wouldn't change the way I feel. The sigh would still be there — I'd simply have chosen not to show it to you. That was the mistake my father made. He knew exactly how to be the person my mother wanted him to be, and he did it for years, because he was kind — and because he loved her, in a way. So she never knew what he was really like at all. She was just given the side of him he knew she'd be happy with.'

'But she *was* happy with it,' Nick pointed out. 'Look at her now, glooming round the place. She hates knowing the truth.'

'That's just the point!' said Sasha. 'Of course she does, because she can see now that she lived for all those years only knowing half of it. She feels she was made a fool of. And she was, although Dad meant it kindly.'

'But she couldn't have accepted the truth,' Nick argued. 'Look what happened when you found out about Laura and made your Dad come clean about it. Your mother fell apart at the seams — and she's still furious with you. I reckon she knew all along that he was seeing someone else. She just didn't want to be told.'

'She *did*!' insisted Sasha. 'Not long before it all happened, she said, "If you found out your father was having an affair, you would tell me, wouldn't you?" And I didn't know what to

45

say, because I already knew he was. That's why I want you to know exactly how I feel about things, all the time, even if you don't always like it. And I want to know how *you* feel. We've got to be honest with each other, Nick. If I didn't care about you, it would just be a game, and it wouldn't matter. But I do.'

Nick stood up and said, 'Think I'll have another cup of tea. You want one?'

'No, thanks,' said Sasha with contempt. 'Go on, then. Run away if you've got to.'

'Seems like a good idea,' said Nick, trying to appear unruffled. He joined the queue for the service counter. What was it about women, he wondered, which made them want to expose their innermost feelings so defencelessly? Was it a kind of shame-game, trading on the male tradition of not hitting a chap when he was down? When someone's defences were as far down as Sasha's, it was like being put in charge of some infinitely fragile, vulnerable thing. You had to take immense care of it, or hand it over to someone else.

The trouble was, he thought as the queue shuffled on, he didn't want to be in charge of anything. He liked Sasha a lot, but he couldn't be committed to her. Or to anything. He squinted up at the sky which sparkled through the leaves of the big trees in the tea enclosure and felt a small whiff of happiness, as distinct as wood-smoke. It was silly to ask for anything more, he thought. There was no certainty.

When he got back to the table, Sasha had got her drawing-book out and was embellishing the sketch she had done in the hot-house. 'Tarting it up,' she announced cheerfully, to Nick's relief. That was the good thing about Sasha. She always knew when things were getting too heavy.

A couple of days later, Len unexpectedly set Nick on stripping down a Vauxhall engine for rebuilding. It was a change from bodywork and routine servicing, and something of a step-up. Usually, Jim or Colin were the only people entrusted with engines apart from Len himself, but Colin was on holiday and Len was busy trying to talk a customer into buying a rusty Datsun. Lanky, monosyllabic Jim was putting a new gearbox in a Peugeot, but he came over from time to time to see how Nick was getting on, standing with his thumbs hooked in the side pockets of his boiler-suit as he watched the orderly boxful of bolts and washers and other small bits and pieces accumulating.

'It's all right,' Nick told him a little irritably. 'I'm not going to break anything or lose anything. I've done lots of bike engines.'

'Bikes aren't cars,' said Jim, and went back to the Peugeot.

Bikes were better, Nick thought. Size for size, they developed far more power. And they were accessible, not like these great crude lumps of metal. Still, he enjoyed his day, despite squashing a finger when a spanner slipped off a nut when he was exerting a lot of leverage on it. He went round to see Sasha feeling reasonably cheerful.

The next morning, cutting through a back street on his way to work, Nick caught up with a police car which was waiting to turn out into the main road at the far end. He pulled up behind it.

The car's near-side door opened and a uniformed figure got out. Nick's heart sank. The policeman came up to him and said, 'Off the bike, lad.' The other man in the car backed it on to the pavement and came across as well. Nick switched off the ignition and heaved the bike on to its stand.

Looking at him accusingly, the policeman said, 'I could hear your engine from inside the car.'

'It's got standard silencers on it,' said Nick with truth.

The policeman walked round the bike slowly, checking the tax disc and bending down to inspect the tyres. He took out his notebook and said, 'Name?'

'Cartwright,' said Nick. 'Look, what's all this about? I've got to get to work.'

'Don't come the stroppy with us,' said the second policeman. 'Where's your driving licence?'

'I don't carry it around,' said Nick.

'Insurance certificate?'

'It's at home.'

'You have *got* one?'

47

'Of course I've got one.'

'What d'you say your name was?'

'Cartwright,' Nick repeated with resignation. 'Dominic Alexander Cartwright.'

It was twenty-five minutes before he got away, the bike having been slowly and minutely inspected and everything from the top box left strewn about on the pavement. Nick had to bring his documents into any police station within seven days, but he hadn't actually been charged with anything.

'You're late,' said Len when he finally arrived at the garage.

'I know,' said Nick. 'Got stopped by the pigs.'

'Don't give me that,' said Len. 'Nice easy excuse, that is.' Nick opened his mouth to protest, but Len went on, 'And if it's true, well, you shouldn't ride so fast. Death on wheels, you are. All adds up to the same thing – you want to get up earlier so's to make sure you get here on time. I'm not paying you to roll in here half an hour late. You can start putting that engine together. Change that cracked piston, and it'll want a new valve. Make sure it's properly ground in. And I hope everything's clean.'

'It's all been through the parts cleaner,' said Nick. What did Len think he was – an idiot?

'All right, smart-arse, get on with it,' said Len.

Nick raged inwardly as he went across to the stores for a piston. It had been the same at school. People in authority spent their whole time putting you down. 'If I want your opinion, Cartwright, I'll ask for it.' As if there were two separate kinds of people, same as there were in Roman times. You could imagine old Green, the Headmaster, up there in a toga, with a wreath of laurel leaves round his head, laying down the law – Len, too, although he'd look bloody silly. While the irks like Nick and Gary scampered around in their little short tunics doing as they were told and hoping not to get flogged or be given to some lion for its breakfast. It was a lousy system. Stupid, too. Toga-people weren't the only ones with ideas.

He forgot his indignation in the interest of assembling the engine. There was a kind of pleasure in the careful application of exactly the right torque, the allowance of exactly the right clearance. The engine took shape slowly, approaching the point where it would once again be a functioning thing, able to support its own life.

Jim came and looked from time to time, his long, sallow face suspicious. Nick ignored him. When he had completed the engine he went in search of Len to tell him that it was done. Jim intercepted him at the office door and said, 'Len's out, test-driving Mr Burton's Allegro. If you've finished, you can put a new spring in that Passat. Near-side, rear.'

'What about the engine?' asked Nick. 'Shall we put it back in the car?' He was dying to see it run.

'You can leave that to me and Len,' said Jim. 'Get that spring done. The bloke's coming for the car straight from work.'

'Okay,' said Nick, shrugging. If he ever ran a business, he thought, he'd make people feel as if they mattered.

The next morning Nick was back on bodywork, grovelling along the side of a Dolomite, rubbing out the rust. He looked across at Jim, who was fitting the rebuilt engine back into the Vauxhall Chevette. How many years had he been in the same job? Thirty? And Len, who was older – forty? It was mind-boggling. And they were so smug about it, too. 'When you've been at this game as long as I have . . . .'

Nick squatted back on his heels and dangled his arms across his knees, letting his head hang down to take the ache out of the back of his neck. What was the alternative to such monotony? He himself had worked in factories, in pubs, in cafés. He had welded and navvied and sand-blasted, painted, window-cleaned, washed up and been paid to smile at idiots who bought things they couldn't afford and didn't need. All work was boring after the first day or two while you found out how it was done. Rebuilding the engine had been pretty good, but things like that didn't come his way often. It would be great to be an actual engineer, trying out new ideas, building prototypes –

'Get on with it,' said Len on his way to answer the telephone which was ringing in the office.

Nick got on with it. 'This valance is ever so fudgy,' he said to Len when he came past on his way back. 'Wouldn't it be better to cut it right out from behind the front wheel and weld a plate in?'

'It's not a bloody Rolls Royce,' said Len. 'The punter wants a cheap respray, and a cheap respray he'll get. And that means a quick respray. Just bung the holes up with filler and get it painted. Don't hang about.'

He went back to the Vauxhall where he had joined Jim and Nick continued to rub dispiritedly at the crumbling Dolomite. Depression was creeping over him like an insidious dampness, spreading a kind of chilling mildew across his mind. Tomorrow and tomorrow and tomorrow, like it said in some Shakespeare play they'd done at school. All the days the same as each other.

In an unusual mood of nostalgia, Nick went on thinking about school as he continued to work automatically. It was a pity, really, that it had been such a mess. Some of it could have been quite interesting if he could only have stopped hating it long enough to pay a bit of attention. Mr Whitnall had been all right – you could see he thought Chemistry was a real turn-on. And Miss Black, up in her art room. But most of them were so bogged down about stupid things like whether you wore jeans or 'proper' trousers that they never got to think of you as a person at all. Just a walking source of irritation. It had been a war. Perhaps, he thought, school came at the wrong time. If he'd known when he was fourteen how crushingly boring work could be, school would have seemed quite a jazz. And as to the lucky bastards who went to College – they had real jam on it. A Government grant to wander around some ivy-clad pile in the dirtiest jeans you liked, while old blokes in frock-coats called you Sir? What a doddle. But then, students were going to be toga-people, weren't they. Nick's depression deepened.

It was pouring with rain at lunch time and Gary sat down on the edge of the hoist with his sandwich box, glancing up at Nick as if assuming that he would do likewise.

'I'm fed up with this place,' said Nick, pushing his arms into his leather jacket. 'I'm going down the caff.'

'Costs money,' said Gary.

'Oh, to hell with it,' said Nick.

He rode off through the rain to Ron's and had the Special. Steak and kidney pie, greens and mash, followed by blackberry crumble and two cups of tea. He had a short argument with a middle-aged man who thought the Japanese had never built anything as good as his old BSA, then started back to the garage. It was still raining.

He pulled up at a zebra crossing for a woman with a pram and hardly realised that anything was wrong when he heard a thud from a little ahead of him as the car on his right failed to stop. Then the woman began to scream and Nick realised that the child beside her, on the far side of the pram, had run ahead into the path of the car. He pulled the bike on to its stand and went to look. The child, a little girl, lay face downward in the road in a transparent pink plastic mac. Her feet were in red wellies and she still clutched an ice-cream cornet in her hand. The blob of white ice-cream it had contained had been flung ahead of her to land on the wet, oily surface of the road. A small puddle of blood was creeping from under her face.

'Oh, Jesus,' said the white-faced driver. 'I didn't see her. I just didn't see her.'

The woman knelt beside the child in the road, screaming, 'Tracey! Tracey!'

Nick parked his bike by the kerb and went across to crouch beside her. 'We'll get an ambulance,' he said gently. 'You'd better not try to move her. Someone ring up,' he said over his shoulder to the ring of spectators.

A despatch rider with the name of his firm emblazoned on his jacket bib came to a halt beside Nick and said, 'Trouble?' Then he saw the child and said, 'Oh, Christ. Anything I can do?'

'You got a radio?' asked Nick.

'Yeah, sure,' said the despatcher. 'I'll call in and get them to dial 999. Hang on.'

The child on the road moved a little and gave a spluttering cry, and her mother dived at her. 'Tracey,' she said. 'Oh, my God, she's all blood, look, somebody do something, oh, God.'

Nick felt utterly helpless. Then a young woman pushed past him firmly and said to the child's mother, 'Don't try and pick

51

her up, dear. Wait until the ambulance comes.'

'On its way,' reported the despatcher.

'Someone give me a coat or something,' said the young woman. The driver of the car which had hit the child produced a checked rug.

'Are you a nurse?' Nick asked the young woman, who was speaking reassuringly to the little girl as she tucked the rug round her.

'I'm a doctor,' she said, glancing up briefly. 'Did you see it happen?'

'Yes,' said Nick. 'More or less.'

'Stick around, then. You'll be wanted.'

It seemed an agonisingly long wait for the ambulance. A long queue of traffic built up behind the stationary car and the crowd of spectators and Nick, for the first time in his life, was immensely glad to see a policeman arrive. The ambulance appeared shortly after that, with calm, cheerful men who collected up the little girl and her mother, together with the pram containing the baby which, strangely enough, had remained peacefully asleep. The despatch rider went on his way and the ambulance drove off and, for the second time in as many days, Nick found himself giving his name and address to the fuzz.

Chapter 6

'You're for it,' muttered Gary as Nick came into the garage.

'I couldn't help it,' Nick protested. 'A little kid was run over, right in front of me. I mean, what would you have done?'

Gary saw Len coming, and disappeared quickly.

'More bloody excuses, I suppose,' Len snarled.

'Look, I really am sorry,' said Nick. 'Honest, it wasn't my fault.'

' 'Course it was your fault,' said Len. 'You rebuilt the damned engine. Why didn't you fill it with oil?'

Nick blinked. There was something else. 'The Vauxhall?' he queried. What had they done?

'Of course, the Vauxhall. You don't build up engines every day, do you? Not that you're going to build any more,' added Len.

'You didn't run it, did you?' asked Nick with dawning horror. 'Not without oil in it?'

'It was your job to fill it with oil,' said Len. 'And you didn't. The blasted thing's seized solid. Big ends, little ends — completely wrecked.'

'But I asked Jim!' said Nick frantically. 'I said, were we going to put it back in the car, and he said to leave it to him and you. If he was going to take over, then why didn't *he* fill — '

'Just shut up!' Len shouted. 'You're not going to smart-talk your way out of this one. Jim says he definitely told you to top it up with oil.'

'Then he's a bloody liar!' Nick shouted back. The child lying in the road, still clutching the empty ice-cream cornet, and the ruined engine which he had so carefully assembled, which should have been running, combined in a wave of anguish. He turned away, casting a bitter glance at the Vauxhall Chevette with its bonnet still open. He came face to face with the disintegrating car on which he had been working so unrewardingly all morning, and his anger boiled over.

'You bastards!' he shouted, and aimed a furious kick at the Dolomite. The reinforced toe of his work-boot went clean through the base of the rusty door panel, leaving a gaping hole.

'Get out!' yelled Len. 'Just get out of this place and don't come back! You're sacked. I'll give Gary your cards and your pay, he can drop them round tomorrow. And don't try for any garage work round here, because nobody'll have you, not by the time they hear what I've got to say.'

It was true. Nick walked out and paused in the forecourt to put his crash helmet on. His fingers felt clumsy. He rode away, then realised that he didn't know where he was going. He turned down a *cul-de-sac* with a pile of sand and a cement mixer at the end, and stopped. Bastards, he thought again, in

53

grief for the engine. They could have taken care.

Suddenly the day seemed very empty. He couldn't go back to Ron's and face the questions and the laughter. Not yet. And Sasha would be at work. Even Maurice was at work, wearing his brown warehouse coat and doling out more or less the right parts in his commercial vehicles store.

Ahead, he knew, lay the familiar pattern of unemployment. The dragging hours, the marking of the passage of the day by cups of tea or by the periodic rolling of a cigarette. Endless time spent sitting in the flat, re-reading bike magazines. After a bit, you didn't care whether you went out or not. After a bit longer, you were too half-dead even to want to. He must fend that off for as long as he could. Keep doing something. He turned the bike round and headed for Croydon.

Being mid-afternoon, the pub was shut. The side gate was bolted, too. Nick looked in vain for a bell, then banged on the saloon door with his knuckles, several times. After a pause, an upstairs window was pushed up and his mother looked out, clutching a dressing gown at her neck. 'Oh,' she said a little reluctantly. 'It's you, love. I'll come down.'

Oh, hell, Nick thought. She's in bed with Tim. Stupid idea to come here. He felt obscurely let down, and immediately despised himself for wanting to rely on his mother, or on anyone. But despising himself made everything worse. At this point, if he didn't have his own approval, he had nothing.

A chain rattled and the door was unlocked and opened. 'You got the sack?' asked Barbie, now in a pink velour tracksuit.

'Yes,' said Nick.

'Thought you must have done, turning up in the middle of the day,' she said, leading the way to the kitchen through the dim, beery-smelling bar. 'We don't see much of you when things are okay.' But she was not complaining. 'Get fed up with it, did you?'

For a moment, Nick felt childishly shaky. He scowled at the cruet sets standing on a stainless steel tray, and tried not to keep remembering the little girl lying in the road, with the blood spreading from under her head.

'Cup of tea,' said Barbie, and put the kettle on. Then she

54

came and hugged him. She seemed very small now, and yet it didn't seem so long since she had been taller than him.

'They're such sods,' he said, and told her all about Len and Jim and the engine, and about being stopped for having a loud exhaust and being late, and about the child being run over.

'Things all happen together, don't they,' said Barbie sympathetically. 'What are you going to do – look for another garage job?'

Nick shrugged. 'Dunno,' he said. There was Len's badmouthing to contend with. And he could already see the cards on the Job Centre boards, mostly for qualified nurses or early-morning cleaners, with a few caretaking posts 'suit retired person'. He didn't even want to think about it.

'We might be able to use a bit of extra help here for a while,' offered his mother. 'I'll ask Tim.'

'No,' said Nick at once. 'I mean, thanks, but I couldn't do that. It wouldn't work, anyway. Tim thinks I'm a yob, and I can't help sending him up.'

'Yeah,' Barbie admitted. 'You two do seem to get the wrong side of each other.' After a pause while she made the tea, she added, 'It's a pity you can't find something more interesting.'

'You need qualifications,' said Nick.

'Suppose so,' his mother agreed. 'But couldn't you go to evening classes or something?'

'Bloody flower-arranging and Yoga,' said Nick, frowning. The thought of sitting at a desk again, staring at a blackboard, filled him with panic.

'People *do*, though,' said Barbie, understanding what he meant. 'Helen did a word-processor course. And Tim says she was hopeless at school.'

'She's just dim,' said Nick, who had met Tim's daughter occasionally and been irritated by her silence. She wore her hair hanging over one eye like Claud did, only Claud looked classy and Helen didn't.

'All the same,' said Barbie defensively, 'she's got quite a good job now, with a firm that imports cheese. Her boss wants her to go to Holland with him, to take notes at meetings.'

'Or something,' said Nick cynically.

'Don't be like that,' said Barbie.

Tim came in, looking as if he had just had a wash and a shave and put on a clean shirt. His thinning hair was neatly brushed back from its bald patch. 'Hello, there!' he said as if Nick was a barful of people. 'How's the world treating you?'

Nick considered several possible answers and said, 'Like a dog-turd, actually.'

'Charming,' said Tim.

Barbie put in quickly, 'Poor old Nick's lost his job.'

'I'm not surprised, if he uses language like that,' Tim remarked. 'However.' Making an effort, he turned back to Nick and said, 'All ready for kick-off, are you? It's the big day on Sunday – your coming-of-age celebration.'

'Don't remind me,' said Nick gloomily.

'Good lord, boy, you're not old enough to start regretting birthdays,' said Tim. 'Wait till you're my age – fat and forty!'

He looked expectant, and Nick knew he was supposed to say something polite about his stepfather's slender and youthful appearance – but he didn't. Perversely, he enjoyed the irritated silence.

Barbie tried again. 'I didn't tell you, Nicky, Tim says we'll meet all the catering expenses.'

'Our present to you,' said Tim.

'Oh,' said Nick without enthusiasm. 'Thanks.' Some present he thought.

'I've made the cake and put the marzipan on, but I won't ice it until the day before,' Barbie went on determinedly. 'Otherwise it gets so hard.'

'Blasted cheek, Dad asking you to do the catering,' Nick said. 'It's not as if you keep in touch or anything.'

'I should hope not,' said Tim, putting his arm round Barbie possessively. 'No, we don't mind doing it. I mean, we can get all the stuff wholesale and it solved the problem of what to give you. Helen says she'd like to come to the party, by the way, her and her boy-friend. I don't think you've met him – Trevor. Works for the Gas Board. You don't mind, do you?'

'No, they're welcome to him,' said Nick.

'More the merrier, if you ask me,' said Barbie hastily, with a nervous glance at Tim, who had removed his arm from her shoulders and was looking exasperated. 'If there's a good old crowd there, it'll make things easier. We don't want just a few of us, trying to make conversation, do we?' She gave Nick a quick wink which he fully understood. She wanted him to behave himself here and now, but she felt exactly the same about the party as he did.

Trying to make amends, he said, 'Never mind. This time next week, the whole ghastly thing will be over.'

'That's all the thanks we get,' said Tim.

Nick decided that the situation needed retrieving, specially as he had rather hoped they would stand him a meal. 'I'll mow your lawn if you like,' he offered. It was a real bind, moving all those metal tables and chairs, but you couldn't mow round them.

'In that case,' said Tim, 'you can stay for a pie and chips.' His eyes were as calculating as the windows in a one-arm bandit, Nick thought. There was always a percentage for the house. 'And next time you feel like dropping in during our time off,' Tim added, 'ring first. Right?'

'Right,' said Nick.

Sasha was deeply and mournfully sympathetic. 'It's so unfair,' she said. 'Isn't there some tribunal you can go to about wrongful dismissal or something?'

'Not a hope,' said Nick. They were sprawling on her bed later the same evening. 'Who'd believe my word against Len's and Jim's? And can you imagine what it would be like if Len was told he had to take me back? Life wouldn't be worth living.'

'I see what you mean,' Sasha agreed. 'But I still think it's rotten.'

Nick shrugged. 'That's the way it goes,' he said. 'Win some, lose some.' Out of the wreckage of the day, an idea had emerged. 'I was thinking,' he added, 'I could do some despatch riding. It's a lot of hassle, but the money's good. That bloke who stopped and radio'd for an ambulance today when that little kid was run over – I thought afterwards, I wouldn't mind

57

doing his job.'

'Awfully dangerous,' Sasha objected.

'No more dangerous than riding to work or coming over here,' Nick pointed out. 'And you don't mind me doing that.' He was feeling much more cheerful. 'The despatch firms have adverts in the *Motor Cycle News* every week. I thought I'd go round some of them tomorrow and see if I can sort something out.'

Sasha leaned forward and twined her arms round his neck. 'You are marvellous,' she said. 'I'd have been shattered if all that had happened to me.'

'I *am* shattered,' said Nick.

Sasha laughed and said, 'No, you're not. Look at you – perfectly normal.'

'That's because it's normal to be shattered,' said Nick. 'You just get used to it.'

He meant it as a joke, but Sasha looked at him with concern. 'You make me want to take care of you,' she said. 'Keep you safe from nasty things happening.'

'Sounds incredibly dull,' said Nick, taking fright. He thought of pipe-and-slippers Gary. Evasive action was called for.

Sasha reached down and picked up a magazine from the floor. 'Suit yourself,' she said, and turned a page.

Nick pitched the magazine across the room. After all, the threat of domesticity was not exactly imminent.

'You'll want a hundred pounds deposit for your radio,' said the woman who ran the despatch firm, 'and your bike expenses are your own affair. How much you earn depends a lot on how well you know London. Most people get in a bit of a muddle at first, but once you start to zip round quickly, you can do a lot of drops in the day, specially when you know most of the places you're sent to. A lot of them are regular customers.'

'Sounds great,' said Nick. 'I'll buy an *A to Z*. I know south London pretty well, and the West End.' And he could just about find the hundred quid deposit, he thought. He'd worked a week in hand at Len's, so there'd be two weeks' wages to come, and with any luck, he might get given a few notes for his birthday.

'Start Monday, then,' said the woman, glancing through her blue-rimmed spectacles at the book in which she had written Nick's name and address. 'I've got all I need to know.'

'What time?' asked Nick.

'Up to you,' she said. 'We're open at eight, but a lot of boys don't start until later, particularly if they've done an out-of-town drop the night before. Or something.' She drooped a green-tinted eyelid.

'I'll be there at eight,' said Nick.

'There's a good boy,' said the woman.

He wasted a bit of time in a record shop, then bought a pizza and a packet of crisps and went to the park where he and Gary usually had their lunch.

Gary came through the gate, looking exactly as Nick knew he would, neat in his quilted anorak, with the pale blue lunch box under his arm and his hands pink from Swarfega and scrubbing. His thin face lit up at the sight of Nick and he said, 'Hello! How are things?'

'Great,' said Nick. 'Just got a job as a despatch rider. Start Monday.'

'Brilliant,' said Gary. 'I thought you might be here. I tried to get the old sod to give me your wage packet to bring, but he wouldn't have it. The wages are all made up, too, but he's just being awkward.'

'He'll be first against the wall,' said Nick. 'Come the revolution. Never mind — long as he coughs it up before the weekend.'

'He'd better,' said Gary. 'Here, we've got some good news! At least, Liz has. She put her name down with a Housing Association ages ago, when she first decided to try and get her own place, then when she knew she was pregnant she wrote and told them. And they've offered her a flat. Isn't it great! It's in one of those old mansion blocks, but they're all due to be modernised.'

'Great,' said Nick automatically. He was not sure what Gary was implying. 'And you're going to live there, too?' he enquired.

'Yep. Getting married, soon as we come back from Sweden.'
Gary sat down on a bench and busied himself with his lunch
box.

'You're off there on Monday?' said Nick through a mouthful
of pizza.

'First thing.'

'I'll be belting round London for Kamakazi Despatch or
whatever they're called,' said Nick. Which was good, he
thought. It would have been super-dreary at Len's with Gary
away.

'Liz says, would you and Sasha like to come round for a
drink on Saturday night,' Gary remembered. 'Tomorrow, that
is. Not too early – she doesn't finish at the restaurant until ten.'

Nick threw a pizza crumb to the sparrows and said, 'Yeah,
'spect so. Thanks.'

'Whaddya mean, you expect so?' demanded Gary indignantly. 'You bloody well better turn up, or Liz'll do her nut.'

'Okay, okay,' said Nick. 'I'll be there. Don't panic.'

'Just you wait,' said Gary with superiority. 'You'll find yourself with responsibilities one day.'

'Not if I can help it,' said Nick.

After Gary had gone back to the garage, Nick sat on in the
windy sunshine, hands linked behind his head and one booted
foot resting on top of the other. The afternoon yawned ahead,
empty. While he had been at Len's, he had so often thought
with envy about the lucky so-and-sos who were free to walk
about idly when he had been wrestling with rusted-in bolts, yet
here he was, on a Friday afternoon with only a couple of days
to go before he started despatching on Monday, and already the
hours were stretching themselves out ominously.

The more you thought about time, he reflected, the bigger it
got. If you went on doing it long enough, it swelled so much
that it crowded everything else out and you just sat there, coun-
ting seconds. He dared not even remember it, for fear that it
might start happening again. His legs and feet felt inert at the
very thought of it. Evasive action was called for. He scored a
good shot into the litter bin with his crumpled paper bag, and

stood up. He would go back to the flat and tidy it up a bit in preparation for the dreaded shindig on Sunday night. The old man had done his bit with the sick green, but he wasn't much good on general squalor.

The sunlight which filtered in through the dusty windows made things look worse. Combined with the scummy-duckpond effect of the walls, it gave the flat a deeply underwater appearance although the place was perched twelve floors up. Nick filled a bucket with water and cleaned the windows, polishing them off with a crumpled newspaper. It was an improvement, but it wasn't a cure. He tidied his room by throwing everything into the cupboard and shutting the door quickly, then came back into the sitting-room and looked at the walls again. If only they were just a bit paler, he thought, it wouldn't be so bad.

Almost before the plan was complete in his mind, he was out of the flat and clattering down the stairs. In the Discount Paint Store he grabbed a shade card and scanned it impatiently. He couldn't paint the flat white as Sasha said it should be — it would take at least three coats to kill that green. It would have to be something near it, then with any luck Maurice wouldn't be too furious. Amendment wasn't as drastic as total change. He took the shade card to a man who was flicking a feather duster across the rows of tins, dabbed his finger on a square called Spring Mist and said, 'Have you got any of that?'

'Matt or silk?' enquired the man.

'Matt,' said Nick after a slight pause. It sounded more business-like. Then he wondered if he'd made one of those dry-sherry mistakes. 'Enough for one room,' he added.

'What size?' asked the man.

He'd already answered that question, Nick thought. 'Whatever size is enough for one room,' he said patiently.

The man rolled his eyes and said, 'What size is the room, dumbo?'

Nick shrugged. This was becoming a game. 'Room-size,' he said gormlessly.

The man folded his arms with the feather duster sticking out from the crook of his elbow and sighed. 'Live in the flats, do you?' he asked.

Nick put on his half-witted face and nodded.

'You'll want half a gallon, then,' said the man. 'None of those flats got very big rooms. And you can always come back if you want some more.'

'Yeah,' said Nick. He checked his change in case he had overdone the village idiot act, and found it twenty pence short. 'Come on,' he said, and the man sighed again and paid up.

Back in the flat, Nick levered the lid off the tin and stared dubiously at the contents. He wished he could ask Sasha whether Spring Mist was tasteful or not. She would undoubtedly know. It was paler than he had expected, a turnip-like shade which reminded him of Gary's face by about half-past eleven at any party. He was a terrible person for throwing up. Nick found a brush and started painting.

The colour Maurice had used was shiny, and the Spring Mist seemed reluctant to stick to it. Streaks of Lime Green showed through, and Nick cursed. It was obviously going to need two coats. He completed one wall and did the bits above and below the windows, then started on the long stretch between them and the door. The flat, chalky smell of the paint made his throat feel dry and he decided to stop and have a cup of coffee before he did the rest of it. He opened the sitting-room window to let some air in and went into the kitchen. Several crates of assorted booze stood on the floor beside the sink. Maurice was evidently taking this party seriously.

Nick stood by the window and stared down at the area of muddy grass behind the flats as he waited for the kettle to boil. An old man walking along the concrete path which bordered the grass paused to rake about in a litter bin, then shuffled on again. Nick wondered if he would ever end up like that. After all, the poor old bloke down there hadn't been *born* old. He'd been a kid, been at school. Had a twenty-first birthday. Did he know he was going to fetch up poking about in litter bins? Probably not. When you're small, Nick thought, you assume you're getting better and better every day, same as you get bigger. But, sooner or later, you were going to reach a time when that stopped, and the process started going the other way.

After that, you'd start getting worse instead, so that you ended up bent and shrunk and senile.

Perhaps, Nick reflected, the rot set in at school. Maybe Those In Charge knew it, and that's why they were always telling you you'd never be any good. By about the fourth year, you started going downhill, and by the time you were twenty-one you'd definitely had it.

He took his coffee into the sitting-room and perched on the table to roll himself a cigarette. Yes, being twenty-one was the beginning of the end. That's why Mature People were so keen to celebrate it. Join the Crumblies Club, son. Welcome aboard. He parked the cigarette in the ashtray Maurice had pinched from the pub, picked up the pot of paint and, in huge Spring Mist letters, painted SENILITY STARTS AT 21 across Maurice's green wall. Then he sat down again and laid the brush across the top of the pot. He stirred his mug of coffee and surveyed the large statement. He rather liked it. After a while, he got up and started work again, filling in the bulk of the wall from ceiling to floor until he reached the painted words. Idly, he worked his way round them, leaving a margin of Lime Green surrounding each of the letters so that they looked even bigger. He would paint them over before Maurice got in, he thought, but he might as well do the end wall first.

The day's events ran through his mind as he finished the end wall. He came to the conversation with Gary in his mental replay, and realised that he'd better ring Sasha about Liz's invitation to go round for a drink tomorrow, before she planned some dire alternative, landing him in the dog-house either with her or Liz. Or both. They were just about as stroppy as each other. He went into the kitchen to see what time it said on the electric cooker's clock, and found that it was nearly six. Sasha would probably be home. She got off early on Fridays, though she often worked on a Sunday. He dialled her number.

Sasha agreed that going for a drink with Liz and Gary would be fine, and said Liz had already asked her. She told him that her mother had decided to accept the offer to play for the ballet class, then she said, 'She's been and had her hair done again, too, ready to cut a dash on Sunday.' Speaking close to the

63

receiver, she added quietly, 'I had to laugh. They've done it what they call Sandalwood, and it's as near as damn it *pink*. Do you remember how she hit the roof when I had mine pink last year?'

'I didn't have much to do with her then,' said Nick cautiously.

'Well, she did,' said Sasha. 'And now she's suddenly got this thing about looking modern and young. It's this expensive place she's going to.'

Nick had a sudden, horrifying fantasy that Mrs Bowman might have fallen into the hands of Claudia, in her capacity as apprentice-hairdresser. The thought of being discussed by those two was blood-chilling. He regretted afresh his impulsive decision to ask Claud to the party.

There was an aggressive silence from the telephone's receiver, then Sasha said, 'Were you listening to me?'

'No,' said Nick. 'Not just then. Sorry — what is it?'

'I was *saying*,' said Sasha, 'that I thought we ought to do something tomorrow to celebrate your birthday, just the two of us. I mean, this party on Sunday, it's very *general*, isn't it? I wondered if we could go somewhere. We could be back in time to go round to Gary's in the evening.'

'Okay,' said Nick willingly. It seemed a good idea. Old Maurice would be doing a hell of a sergeant-major act tomorrow about his party, and a good excuse to be out of the place would be welcome.

'Let's go to the seaside,' said Sasha eagerly. 'The weather's still nice — and it isn't too far, is it?'

'Only an hour on the bike,' said Nick. 'Great. Let's go early. What if I pick you up at nine?'

'Lovely!' said Sasha. 'Where shall we go? Mum says she used to like Broadstairs, but it might be fun to go somewhere noisier — real candyfloss and fun-fairs.'

They discussed the merits of various seaside places for some time, and then Nick heard Maurice's key in the lock. Damn, he thought. He'd meant to get those letters painted over. 'See you at nine,' he said quickly. 'Got to go. The old man's just come in.' And he hung up.

Chapter 7

Maurice came into the room and stopped, thunderstruck. 'What are you doing?' he said. 'What the *hell* are you doing?' His astounded gaze took in the green-rimmed letters which proclaimed, SENILITY STARTS AT 21, two feet high on the streaky Spring Mist wall, and his mouth hung open.

'It's all right,' Nick assured him. 'I'm going to paint over it.'

'Paint it over, be damned,' said his father. 'You're going to scrub it off. The whole bloody lot of it. I did this room Lime Green, and Lime Green it's going to stay. Now, get a bucket and get started.'

Nick took a deep breath. 'Look,' he said, controlling his temper carefully, 'I know it's a bit much, changing it without asking you, but honestly, Dad, people would laugh. I mean, it was great of you to do it, but that rotten cabbage colour really is terrible. I'm not surprised Terry had it by him. It must have been a factory reject.'

'You don't know what you're talking about,' retorted Maurice. 'That green is tasteful. You go up West and see what colours they got there, in all these classy restaurants. Brown. And lamp-shades made of wicker-work. Not that I'd like those myself, can't see what you're eating, but there you are. That's class. Those people, if they have a glass of water it comes out of a bottle and it's got a slice of lemon in it. They know what they want.'

'Brown isn't green,' Nick objected.

'It's the same sort of thing!' protested Maurice. 'I was in a pub in Chelsea last week with the darts team. Real classy pub. They had green walls — darker than these, they were, proper bottle green, with a lot of them little hunting pictures, horses jumping over streams and that. And there was American tourists in there, thought it was marvellous. 'Course, the Yanks,

65

they got nothing like that. One of them said to me, "You British have quality," he said. "Real quality." He took a photo of Terry and me. Bought us a pint.'

'And a whisky?' said Nick, knowing his father's drinking habits.

'And a whisky. *What's that got to do with it?*' bellowed Maurice, infuriated at falling into the trap. 'I'm telling you, just get that muck off the walls.'

'Can't,' said Nick flatly. 'Most of it's dried on. I'll finish it, and give it another coat later tonight.'

'No, you won't,' said Maurice. 'You'll do as you're bloody well told. Scrub off as much as you can, and if it needs another coat of anything, it'll be Lime Green. There's a bit left.'

'Stuff that,' said Nick, exasperated. 'I haven't bought half a gallon of paint to have it going down the sink.' He grabbed the brush and stuck it in the pot then approached the wall with a dripping brushful. Maurice snatched it from his hand and hurled it through the open window.

'You stupid bugger,' said Nick, and began to laugh.

Maurice hit him across the side of the face.

Nick gasped. His fists were clenched and Maurice had flung an arm across his own face defensively. A few long seconds went by, then Maurice said cautiously, 'Don't be silly, now. I didn't mean it – you know that.'

Nick walked out of the room. His face was stinging, but it wasn't that. His own fury was what frightened him. He took his jacket and crash helmet, and left the flat, closing the front door very quietly behind him. When he got down to ground level, some children had found the brush and were daubing Spring Mist on the lift doors.

'Cup of tea,' said Nick. 'Please.' Somehow, he didn't feel like eating. He got out his tobacco tin and papers.

'What you been up to?' asked Ron. 'That's a nasty mark you got on your face.'

'Collided with a lamp post,' said Nick.

'Careless,' said Ron, and put a packet of biscuits on the saucer with Nick's tea. 'There you are,' he added. 'On the

66

house.'

'Ta,' said Nick, stirring. He moved the packet on to the table to keep it dry.

A group of youngsters came in and one of them noticed Nick and said, 'Hi!' Nick recognised him as Stevie Brent, the boy with the C 50, and asked, 'Bike going all right?'

Stevie beamed and said, 'Yes, great. It's lucky I've met you, actually. I ought to have kept your address. Do you know anything about cars?'

'Should do,' said Nick. 'I work at a garage. Or used to.'

'My brother's got this Triumph Spitfire,' said Stevie. 'And he can't get it started.' He gazed at Nick hopefully.

'Is he there now?' asked Nick.

Stevie grinned. 'Oh, yes,' he said. 'He won't have gone anywhere. When I came out he'd got half of it spread over the garage floor.'

'I'll give him a look,' said Nick, sipping his tea. 'Here. Have a biscuit.' And he pushed the packet across the table.

The Spitfire turned out to be suffering from a dud condenser, but Nick knew a motor spares shop which stayed open late, so he bought a new one and fitted it. The Spitfire roared into life, and Paul Brent shouted, 'Marvellous! I thought the carburettor was up the spout.'

Nick shook his head and smiled. He wasn't going to include a lecture on car electrics with the cost of the job, but he quite liked Paul, red-haired and untidy in an unravelling sweater.

'I was going down to Greenwich for a drink,' said Paul. 'I know a couple of blokes there who are into old sports cars. D'you want to come?'

'Why not?' said Nick.

It turned out to be a cheerful evening. Paul and his friends Roger and Phil were students, doing Sociology at a Polytechnic. When Nick first found this out he wished he had not come. This clever lot were likely to talk about things he wouldn't understand, he thought, and he'd feel a complete prat. But, to his surprise, they turned out to be as generally disrespectful of

67

everything as he was. They laughed a lot and drank large quantities of beer, then they all went and had a curry and fetched up at midnight in the house which Roger and Phil shared with a couple of other students, drinking vodka with apple juice.

'I've got to get up in the morning,' said Nick a little indistinctly at somewhere around half past two.

'Work?' asked Roger. He was playing something formless on a guitar.

'No,' said Nick. 'Girl friend. Think I'm going to Brighton with her. Or somewhere.' It all seemed very remote. Paul was lying flat on his stomach on a floor cushion, with his arms out beside him, hands palm up. He looked like a beached penguin.

'Can't think about things like tomorrow,' said Phil. 'Not on.'

'Might never come,' said Nick, and poured himself another vodka. He felt very wise and sad. It was all extremely enjoyable.

He woke the next morning to find the sun streaming in through the curtainless windows. His head hurt when he moved it and he felt stiff from sleeping on a sofa in his clothes, but he was warm and inert, deeply disinclined to move. Paul rolled over on his floor cushion and yawned.

'Oh, Christ,' said Nick, suddenly remembering. 'What's the time?'

Paul peered blearily at his watch and said, 'Twenty to ten.'

Nick groaned. He was marooned in a house in Greenwich, with the bike miles away in Paul's back yard. 'Is there a telephone?' he asked.

'In the hall,' said Phil sleepily. 'Coin-op.'

Nick heaved himself off the sofa and tottered out to ring Sasha. He only had one ten-pence piece.

'You weren't at home,' she said accusingly.

'No. I'm in Greenwich.'

'*Greenwich*? But what on earth –'

He explained briefly what had happened, and said, 'I'll be over as soon as I can – all right?'

'I suppose so,' said Sasha. 'Your father's in a nasty temper. I rang your number to see if you'd overslept, and he just about blew my head off. Ranting on about some wall.'

68

'Ah,' said Nick. 'Yes, he would.' A rapid pip-pip-pip prevented any further conversation and he added, 'Won't be long!' and put the phone down. Then he went to set about the task of getting Paul up and into the Spitfire.

Brighton was rather good, smelling of chips and the sea, with the sparkling expanse of water lying beyond the pier.

'You know you said I ought to get a bike,' said Sasha as they walked along the prom eating violently-coloured ice lollies. 'Well – I really think I will.'

'A 125,' Nick agreed.

'I tried ringing you last night, but there was no answer,' Sasha went on, 'and I thought, yes, it's all right for you, coming and going as you please. Same this morning – there I was, stuck in the house, waiting for His Lordship to come and collect me. I'm sick of being dependent on someone else all the time. It's like being the little woman in a weather-house, waiting for the sunshine of your presence so that I can come out.'

'I'll help you find a bike if you like,' Nick offered. 'And give it the once-over. You don't want to buy a load of rubbish.'

'No,' agreed Sasha. 'I was talking to Dad about it last night. When you weren't in, I went over to see him and Laura. He said if I couldn't quite afford to buy a bike, he'd make up the difference.'

'Lucky old you,' said Nick. 'Are you going to buy a new one, then?'

'Oh, no,' said Sasha. 'It would have to be a second-hand one.'

'We'll have a look through the paper when we get home,' said Nick.

Sasha hesitated. 'I do want it to be *my* bike,' she said. She dropped her lolly stick into a bin and licked her fingers. 'So I might go and look at one or two on my own.'

'Suit yourself,' said Nick, affronted. 'Don't blame me if you get stitched up.'

Sasha laughed. 'I knew you'd go all huffy,' she said. 'It's all right – I shan't buy one without wheeling you in as the technical expert, but I just don't want to tag along being "the girl friend" while you decide on my behalf which bike I should have.'

'Huh!' said Nick. 'Getting stroppy.'

'Just a bit stroppy,' Sasha agreed. 'It's about time.'

Nick stared across the sea to the different shade of blue where the sky began, and wondered why he felt so impatient. All this intricate detail about how people felt was too much to cope with. And tomorrow was the dreaded party. 'Doesn't this town have a fun-fair?' he asked. 'I want to go on a Big Dipper.'

Sasha tucked her arm through his. 'Then we'll go and find one,' she said. She sounded like a mother placating a fretful child.

It was late by the time they got home and, at Sasha's insistence, they went straight round to Gary's house.

Liz opened the door and said triumphantly, 'Ta-rah!' She pointed to the table in the room behind her.

'Good God,' said Nick faintly. Surrounded by plates of savouries and glasses, and backed by a large number of bottles, was a cake in the shape of a motor bike. The engine and wheels were outlined in piped icing and studded with silver balls for the heads of bolts and nuts. White candles were packed closely together to represent a headlight, with red ones at the tail.

'Oh, Liz, it's turned out beautifully!' said Sasha, hugging her friend. 'You are clever!' And Gary was beaming like a proud father, Nick thought. He had no idea what to say about the cake. He felt completely winded by the whole thing.

'I don't think you ought to cut it,' said Gary's mother practically as Nick and Sasha discarded jackets and helmets. 'Not here. Keep it for the party tomorrow and show it off a bit. You never know, love,' she added to Liz, 'there might be some posh people there who'd remember a cake like that. You can do a nice little private line in cakes, you know, once you've got the baby and you're not working. I made one like a big seven for Gary on his seventh birthday, and I did several up and down the street after that. He wanted an eight the next year, but I couldn't do that, not with loaf tins, so I did him an engine with cotton wool for the steam.'

70

'No, I made it for tonight,' said Liz firmly. 'I was going to do a meal for us all, so we're having this instead. You don't know any posh people anyway, do you, Nick?'

Nick thought uneasily of Claudia and shook his head.

'You've completely stunned him, Liz!' said Sasha, laughing. 'Go on, Nick – light the candles. It's very nearly your birthday. We can start celebrating.'

Gary pulled the foil off a bottle of Asti and said, 'Get a glass ready, Liz!'

The cork popped and Mrs Weston squealed and Nick felt a kind of panic. This was the kind of thing he had hoped to avoid. He caught Sasha's eye and gave a faintly apologetic shrug, 'Cheers!' he said as Gary handed him a foaming glass.

'Many happies, dear,' said Mrs Weston. Liz was lighting the absurd clusters of candles. Nick drank half his glass of fizzy wine, burped, and decided that this was okay. Nobody expected anything. They were just friends. And this looked like being another heavy night. Gary was already opening another bottle.

Chapter 8

Mrs Weston's Put-U-Up was more comfortable than the sofa in the Greenwich house had been, and Nick slept until late the next morning. Even then, he barely surfaced to hear Mrs Weston saying something to Liz about trying a dry biscuit, and sank back into a dream about a dripping forest whose leathery leaves impeded him as he tried to ride through it on the bike. Sasha lay beside him with her cheek pillowed on her hand.

Some time later, Gary came in, yawning, and parted the curtains to let in a shaft of sunlight. 'Happy birthday,' he said. 'Want some coffee?'

Sasha burrowed under the blanket like a light-hating mole then said, 'M'm,' and started to wake up. She turned on her back, a hand across her eyes, and said, 'What's the time?'

'Getting on for twelve,' said Gary.

Nick didn't care. This seemed the ideal way to spend the day, in bed with Sasha. She turned to him and kissed him. 'Happy birthday,' she murmured, and wriggled herself into a newly comfortable position with her arm across his chest and her face in his neck.

'You don't want coffee?'

'Oh, we do, we do,' said Sasha without moving. 'We want everything. We'll be up in a minute. Won't we, Nick?'

Nick grunted vaguely. The forest. He could get through all right if he just had a big knife, one of the sort shaped like a slice of melon. And then there was one in his hand, and he was slashing at the creepers which hung on either side of the bike . . . .

'Don't go to sleep again,' Sasha said in his ear. 'Mum's expecting us for lunch.'

'Oh, no,' said Nick.

'Gary!' Mrs Weston's voice from the kitchenette was brisk. She had obviously been up for hours. 'There's some toast here if you want it. I'm just popping round the shops.'

'Okay, Mum,' Gary called back. 'Thanks.'

It was no good. Reality had spread its chill over the day. The Put-U-Up had lost its wonderful comfort and the blanket felt rough over Nick's naked shoulder. He extended an arm and fished about vaguely for his shirt.

The house was a narrow terraced one, with a small back room behind the one in which Nick and Sasha had been sleeping. Here, a few minutes later, Nick found Liz sitting at the table, her hands clasped round a cup of milkless tea. She looked very pale. 'Morning,' she said.

'Are you all right?' asked Nick.

'Sick,' said Liz. 'Be better soon. It's only in the mornings. At least, that's when it's worst.'

Gary emerged from the kitchenette with the toast and said, 'They say it only lasts for the first three months.'

'Only!' said Liz.

'I'm glad blokes don't have babies,' said Nick, and went through the tiny kitchen to the bathroom which had been built on behind it, sticking out into the small garden. Liz's baby was

72

a real thing already, he thought, making its presence felt, changing the lives of its parents. There was some shampoo on the shelf over the basin and he washed his hair, looking at himself in the mirror as he rubbed it dry. Blue eyes, dark eyebrows, wide mouth. 'Bigmouth Cartwright', as old Green used to call him at school. He ran Gary's electric razor over his face, knocked it out in the bin and put it back on the shelf.

When he came out, there was a large, bulky parcel wrapped in brown paper in the middle of the table. Sasha and Liz and Gary were all smiling at him. 'This is our present,' said Gary. 'From me and Liz.'

'Mine's at home,' said Sasha.

The brown paper was sellotaped together loosely, more as a disguise than a packaging, and Nick tore it off quickly to reveal a pair of throw-over motor cycle pannier-bags. 'Oh, marvellous!' he said. 'I'll be able to take quite big parcels. Brilliant! Thanks a lot.'

Gary and Liz beamed at each other, pleased. 'Have some toast, Nick,' said Liz. 'And I'll make some more coffee.'

Mrs Weston came in through the front door and fished a two-ounce pack of tobacco out of her basket. 'There you are, love,' she said. 'No sense in wrapping it.' Brushing aside his thanks, she added, 'What about dinner? You two staying?'

'No, we've got to go home,' said Sasha. 'My mother's invited Nick to lunch. In fact, I'd better ring her, if you wouldn't mind, to say we're on our way. She might be wondering where we've got to.'

'Help yourself, dear, phone's in the hall,' said Mrs Weston, and went to put her shopping away.

'Bad luck about the lunch with Mrs Misery,' Gary said to Nick as Sasha went out to the hall.

Nick shrugged. 'She'll be all right,' he said. 'It's better than going back to the flat. I had a row with the old man, Friday night. Haven't been back since. Better to keep out of the way.'

'Oh, dear,' said Liz. 'Did it get violent?'

Nick scowled. He had been trying not to think about it.

'*He* did,' he admitted. 'I just walked out. Couldn't handle it.'

'You'd think he'd know better, after what happened that other time,' said Gary. 'And that was ages ago, not long after

73

your mother left. You weren't much more than a kid then. You'd really damage him now, if you lost your temper.'

'That's why I walked out,' said Nick.

'What happened the other time, then?' asked Liz.

'I just got fed up with being clipped round the ear,' said Nick, reluctant to remember it. 'And he wouldn't let me out of the door one evening when I was going to take some girl out.' Not Claud — it had been that little dark one with the mole on her cheek, Tanya. 'He stood in front of the door and he kept pushing me in the chest and saying how I couldn't knock the skin off a rice pudding. And I hit him. I thought I'd killed him.'

'He caught his chin on the table on his way down, though,' put in Gary. 'It wasn't all your fault. I'd love to have seen it, though,' he added, grinning. 'Talk about David and Goliath! Things were better after that, though, weren't they.'

'For a while,' Nick conceded. 'I think he just hadn't realised I'd grown up. Nor had I. Scared me to death. 'Course, he was pretty pissed at the time.'

Sasha came back and said, 'That's all right. She sounds calm and cheerful. Well, fairly. We'd better go, though.'

Liz looked at Nick critically and said, 'I think Gary had better lend you a clean shirt, if you're going out to lunch.'

Gary was smaller than Nick, but the slightly tight shirt looked rather smart. Nick borrowed a silk scarf as well, and tucked it into the neck. Gary had snazzy tastes in clothing.

'Oh, *very* presentable!' said Sasha when he went downstairs. 'You look like something out of *Horse and Hound*!'

'Frightfully natty,' said Nick in a caricatured Hooray Henry accent. He picked up the pannier-bags and added, 'Let's go and fit these on the jolly old steed, what?'

Laughing, they all went out of the front door.

The bike was not there.

Nick saw Sasha put her hands over her face. He ran into the middle of the road and stared up and down it in the useless hope that someone had simply moved the bike somewhere else. The pannier-bags were heavy over his arm.

'Oh, *shit*,' he said.

He had been caught out. Again and again he had thought

about the possibility of the bike being stolen, had looked down from the flat to where it was parked in the street below, trying to arm himself against it happening. But it had gone when he was unguarded, not even thinking about it. Having a good time. As if it was a punishment.

Sasha was crying. 'Come on,' he said, putting his arm round her. 'It's only a bike. There's plenty more. I'll get the insurance money.' In about a year, he thought, and about a quarter of what it was worth. A load of bloody sharks *they* were.

'You'd better ring the fuzz,' said Liz sensibly. 'They might have found it. People take bikes for joy rides.'

Sasha blew her nose and said, 'I'll have to let Mum know. It'll take ages to get there by bus, and I said we were on our way.'

'Don't worry about that,' said Gary. 'I'll run you across in the car.' They all trailed back into the house.

'It must have been gone when I went out shopping,' Mrs Weston lamented when they told her what had happened. 'I never thought to look. I am sorry, dear.'

'It doesn't matter,' said Nick.

They stopped at the police station on the way to Sasha's house, and Nick went in to report the disappearance of the bike. The desk sergeant was very polite and kept calling him 'Sir'. It was a complete contrast to the time Nick had taken in his documents after the business of the noisy exhaust, and it puzzled him until he realised that he looked a very different person in his neat shirt and tucked-in scarf, with newly-washed hair. Lesson One, he thought. Always play the Class Game in a cop-shop. Somebody could make a good thing of selling Lingua-phone cassettes to teach people the *Horse and Hound* accent.

Sasha's mother gave him a ten-pound record token and com-miserated about the bike as she poured him a large dry sherry. He noted that her much-bouffed pinky-brown hair looked like a wig, but felt no inclination to laugh. Sasha produced a parcel wrapped in gaily-striped paper. 'This is so awful,' she said wretchedly as she gave it to him. 'I wish there'd been time to change it, but there wasn't. And you will get another bike.' The parcel contained a very good pair of gauntlets, and silk inners to go with them.

'Great,' said Nick. 'Thanks ever so much. They're really good ones. Yes, I'll get another bike.' But not for a long time, he thought. There would be no despatching job now, and you couldn't save up any money on the DHSS.

'I did melon for a starter,' said Joanna. 'I do hope you like it, Nick. Will you open the wine for me, dear?'

'Sure,' said Nick. Things must be bad, he thought. She'd never called him dear before.

The meal passed in a daze. Nick felt as if he was being governed by auto-pilot. He seemed to be behaving all right, but it was nothing to do with him. His real self was still standing in the road outside Gary's house, staring in disbelief at the space where the bike should have been. The emptiness seemed huge and internal, a terrible absence where there had once been mobility and independence and self-respect.

Chapter 9

As the afternoon wore on, Nick began to think uneasily about Maurice. He had not seen him since the Spring Mist episode on Friday, and the old git would be getting properly wound up about this party. He would no doubt have restored the walls to the hideous green. Perhaps Barbie and the oh-so-genial Tim had arrived with a lot of sausages on sticks.

Then something else struck him. If the police had any news of the bike, they would ring up the flat, because that was the number he had given them. It was no use sitting here. He got to his feet and said, 'I'd better be off.'

Sasha and her mother both looked at him reproachfully and he realised that he had interrupted one of Mrs Bowman's long-winded narratives about her student days. He explained his sudden thought about the police and Sasha said, 'Oh, I do hope they've found it.'

'Probably not,' he said, trying to arm himself against disappointment. 'It most likely got picked up and bunged in a van. Professional job. Thanks very much for lunch, Mrs Bowman. See you later, okay?'

'I do think we might be on Christian name terms by now,' said Joanna. 'What time are you expecting people to arrive this evening?'

Nick shrugged and said, 'Whenever you like. Not too early.'

'Shall I come with you now and help get things ready?' Sasha asked him.

'No, thanks,' said Nick firmly. He wasn't sure what sort of mood Maurice would be in, and he certainly didn't want Sasha there if the row should happen to continue. 'Besides,' he said as she looked downcast, 'your mother won't know the way to the flat tonight without you in the car to show her.'

Joanna smiled in wan gratitude, and Nick left to get the bus.

The flat was strangely quiet. Nick frowned as he closed the front door behind him. Maurice usually spent Sunday afternoon watching sport on the television. Where had he got to? Nick looked in the living-room.

SENILITY STARTS AT 21, the wall announced silently. Nick had forgotten how big the letters were. He felt a moment's grudging admiration for Maurice. To leave the wall unchanged was a master-stroke. Ball in Nick's court. Now he'd get the full shock-horror reaction from the people coming to the terrible party. See if I care, he thought defiantly. Good try, Dad, but if anyone's going to be embarrassed, it'll be you, not me.

He found his father in bed, lying flat on his back and snoring heavily. There was an empty whisky bottle on the floor beside him, and the small room stank overpoweringly of alcohol and of Maurice. Nick shook him by the shoulder cautiously and said, 'Dad. You'd better wake up.'

Maurice's snore caught in his throat and he gagged slightly and spluttered. Then the snoring started again. Nick opened the window, with some difficulty as it had been shut for years, and went into the kitchen to make some strong coffee. The place was a wreck. The dirty dishes of three days' meals were piled on the draining board and in the sink, together with a lot of empty bottles. The crates which had contained the drink for the party were seriously depleted. Maurice had clearly gone on a binge.

Nick washed a mug and made some powerful coffee for his father, then took it to the bedroom. 'Listen,' he said more loudly, 'you'll have to wake up. There'll be people here for the party soon. Come on.'

'Piss off,' said Maurice thickly.

'Dad, have the police rung?' Nick asked. 'My bike's been stolen.'

After a pause, Maurice said, 'No.'

Nick left the coffee within his father's reach and went back to the kitchen to tackle the washing up. It took a long time. As he worked, he cursed himself for not coming back sooner. He shouldn't have left him with all that booze. It was asking for trouble. But, for God's sake, the man wasn't a kid, was he? Did he have to be watched over the whole time?

Nick's indignation deepened as he cleaned the sink and the splash-back and wiped the work-top. The cooker was filthy but there wasn't time to tackle that. He mopped the floor, squeezing out the mop in a sinkful of soapy water, then had to clean the sink again because of the scummy detritus it left. Then he discovered that Maurice had at some point been sick in the bathroom. By the time he had cleared that up, and cleaned the basin and put some bleach down the toilet, he was furious. He burst into his father's bedroom and shouted, 'Wake up, will you!'

Maurice's eyes were open, though the coffee stood untouched on the chair beside the bed. He tried to say something without success, and rubbed a hand over his stubbly face.

'What?' demanded Nick, approaching.

With a feeble gesture, Maurice muttered, 'Chrissake shut the window.'

'No,' said Nick. 'The place stinks. What did you have to go and get drunk for?'

'Sorry,' said Maurice. He turned his head slightly on the

78

pillow and winced. 'Oh, Christ. Sorry, boy.'

'Drink your coffee,' said Nick, and went back to the kitchen. A few minutes later he heard his father's stumbling rush to the bathroom. He hoped he was neater about it this time.

There was a ring at the doorbell. Nick went to answer it and found Barbie, barely able to see over a piled armful of catering tins topped by something in a carrier bag. 'Happy birthday, love,' she said cheerfully, indicating the carrier with her chin. 'Little something from me.'

'Thanks,' said Nick. He relieved her of the tins and put them down on the hall table. The carrier bag contained a red sweater with a row of fat white sheep round the bottom.

'Daft, really,' said his mother as he held the sweater up against him. 'Just a bit of fun. Looks as if it'll fit you all right. Where's your dad?'

'In the khazi,' said Nick. 'Thanks for the sweater. It's great.'

'Tim's getting the rest of the stuff out of the car,' said Barbie. She caught a glimpse of Maurice tottering from the bathroom back to his bedroom and said, 'My God. He looks rough.'

'He's been on a three-day binge,' said Nick.

'That's all we need,' said Barbie. They went into the living-room and she stopped, amazed, and stared at the wall. She began to laugh.

'I was going to paint it over,' said Nick, 'but I didn't get it finished.' Even to himself, it sounded lame. He put the catering tins down on the kitchen table. There wasn't going to be enough booze, he thought, not now Maurice had been at it.

Tim came in through the open front door, laden, and stared at the wall in his turn. 'I suppose that's meant to be funny, is it?' he said, depositing more tins. 'Puts us in our place, doesn't it, Barbie? Geriatrics.'

'I didn't mean you,' said Nick. He refrained from making any further excuses. He would just have to live with it.

Tim looked round him with distaste. 'The place could do with a clean-up,' he said.

You should have seen it an hour ago, Nick thought.

Maurice appeared at the door, holding himself very upright,

79

like a man trying to appear at ease in unknown territory. He gave no sign of recognising his ex-wife, but smiled at the people in his living-room with glassy joviality. 'Ah,' he said in the voice of a sergeant imitating an officer, 'do sit down. Make yourselves at home. Nick, don't just stand there. Give everyone a drink.' He made his way unsteadily into the kitchen.

Tim raised his eyebrows eloquently but nobody said anything. Barbie went over to the window and stared down into the street. In her metallic turquoise dress with the big bow on the shoulder, she looked absurdly exotic. Her mass of dark hair was pinned up with silver clips. Nick went across to her, but she did not look up at him. 'I shouldn't have come, Nicky,' she said. 'It's going to be awful. I should never have let him talk me into it.'

Nick gave a short laugh. 'Neither should I,' he said.

He had to hand it to Tim. He had never liked him much, but despite Tim's bland professional-landlord manner, he got down to cleaning and organising the flat with immense efficiency. Maurice switched the television on and sat watching it, tieless and unshaven, with an undrunk mug of tea in his hands, while people vacuumed round him and shifted the furniture about to provide a table near the kitchen for food, with chairs grouped together for conversation and the drinks situated at a safe distance from the record player. Maurice, without moving, ended up as a one-man island, isolated in front of the television set, with his back to everything that was going on.

'There's a hell of a lot of empties in this kitchen,' said Tim. 'He must have had his friends in, by the look of it. Where d'you put your rubbish, Nick?'

'There's a chute, but it's always blocked,' said Nick. 'I'll take it down to the bins.' He gathered up the kitchen bucket and three carrier bags full of empty bottles and went out. Luckily, some people were just getting into the lift, so he joined them. Downstairs, he pushed the rubbish into the evil-smelling bins in their cupboard behind the louvred doors and came out with the empty bucket. He looked along the street, and it hurt afresh not to see the bike parked there.

A stout man with a woman in a fur coat holding his arm was walking along the pavement towards the flats and he waved when he saw Nick. 'Evening!' he said in a double-chinned voice. 'Can you tell me where to find number 712 in this rabbit warren?'

It was the number of Nick's own flat, and he knew who the people were: his rich aunt and uncle, Enid and Walter. He had a wild desire to say he had never heard of number 712. The nightmare party was actually coming true. He swallowed hard. 'I live there,' he admitted.

'Good God, yes,' said the man. 'You must be Nick. I'm your Uncle Walter. And this is Enid.'

'I know,' said Nick. 'I remember you from that funeral.'

Enid said, '*Frightful* affair.' She eyed Nick accusingly and added, 'You've grown.'

Nick wished he was not holding the kitchen bucket, with its residual slick of baked bean juice and cigarette ash. 'I couldn't help it,' he said. 'Dwarfism doesn't run in the family.'

'Oh, witty,' said Enid with distaste. She clutched her fur coat at the neck as if expecting imminent attack.

'Hardly have known you,' said Walter unnecessarily. 'You're in cars these days, I believe?'

'In and out,' said Nick.

'You wouldn't know why my BMW's brake lights have packed up, I suppose?' asked Walter.

'*Such* a nuisance,' said Enid. 'A man in a van pulled up beside us at traffic lights, and he told us.'

'Nice of him,' remarked Nick.

'Nice be damned,' said Walter. 'He called me a steaming prat. I've tried several garages on the way here, but every blasted one of them is shut.'

'It is Sunday,' Nick pointed out. 'Where's the car?'

'Along the road a bit,' said Walter. 'I think they're a bit safer if you leave them under a lamp post. Deters vandals.'

And the best of luck, thought Nick.

The BMW turned out merely to have a blown fuse and, since there were two spare ones at the end of the row, mending it was no problem.

'That's what I call service,' said Walter approvingly as Nick locked the car and handed him the key. 'Most of these garage people would have put that down as a three-hour job. I know what goes on.' He winked with a knowing sideways jerk of his head, and put his arm round Nick's shoulders as they walked back along the pavement. Nick felt faintly nauseated.

He took them up to the flat in the lift, after a long wait. It was obvious that they couldn't walk up twelve flights of stairs, or Walter would have followed his car's example and blown a fuse.

'Guess who's here?' cried Enid coyly as Nick opened the door of the flat.

'Oh, hello, love,' said Barbie, embracing her sister and patting Walter on the arm. 'You're the first. Maurice, stand up and say hello!' she instructed her ex-husband sharply. He, startled by the sudden command, stumbled to his feet and held out his hand, letting go of his still-full mug of tea.

'Oh, bloody marvellous,' said Tim, and went to get a mop.

'Gin and tonic?' suggested Barbie with a determined smile. 'There's no ice yet, I'm afraid, but I've put some in.'

'Perhaps a Cinzano, then,' said Enid. 'If you've got it.'

'Spot of whisky for me,' said Walter, eyeing Maurice dubiously as Tim mopped the floor round their feet.

Nick decided to rescue his father. 'Dad hasn't been feeling too well,' he said. 'Come on, Dad, time you got changed and had a shave.'

He propelled the unresisting Maurice into his bedroom, where he sat down with a groan on the unmade bed and said, 'I feel terrible.'

Nick, hunting for a presentable shirt, almost told him it served him right, but, against all reason, he felt more kindly disposed towards his father at this moment than he had done for years. The silly old bugger had let himself in for all this out of a determination to do the right thing – but Maurice hadn't got it in him to do anything right. And he hadn't got the courage to do things wrong, and to hell with the consequences. And now, he and Nick together, as joint householders of this grotty and unloved flat, were defending it from the critical gaze

82

of the outsiders who were descending on it.

Maurice shuffled off to the bathroom and emerged looking ghastly but cleaner, and struggled into the shirt which Nick had found. He knotted his tie, chin jutting as he looked in the mirror. 'We used to have some binges in the Army,' he said. 'Hardly stand up the next morning – but we had to, of course. Three days' jankers if you couldn't get it right on parade.'

'Yes,' said Nick. His sympathy began to ebb. Music was coming from the living-room. 'I'll go and see what's going on,' he said. 'You won't go to sleep again, will you?'

'I don't need you to tell me what to do,' retorted Maurice. Then, as Nick reached the door, he added, 'Sorry about the bike.'

'Thanks,' said Nick.

In the living-room, Barbie and Tim were entertaining Walter and Enid with professional ease, chatting to them and offering bits of cheese and pineapple on sticks. Nick noticed that Tim had distributed small cards here and there among the dishes on the table. They said, 'T and B Catering. Your party is our pleasure.' What a name for a firm, Nick thought. It sounded like the last fling before you coughed yourself to death. Surprising Barbie hadn't spotted it. But she was funny about Tim. Seemed determined to protect him from the effects of humour.

Walter got to his feet when he noticed Nick and said heartily, 'Here's the birthday boy!' Enid held up a present wrapped in flowered paper, smiling like the Queen Mother, and Walter fished in his pocket for his cheque book, then put his glasses on. Nick pulled the paper off the parcel and revealed a pair of silver-backed hair brushes. Stupid, he thought, but floggable. 'Thank you,' he said.

'Since you've got the family hair,' said Enid, eyeing his un-ruly mop, 'I thought they'd be just what you need.' Who was she kidding, Nick thought. Outside, she hadn't even known who he was. Her own version of the family hair was bleached creamy-white, but her eyebrows and eyelashes were as dark as Barbie's.

Walter signed the cheque with a violent to-and-fro of his pen, tore it out of the book and handed it to Nick. 'For fixing my car,' he said. 'Much appreciated.'

Nick saw to his surprise that the cheque was made out for fifty pounds. 'Don't be daft,' he said. 'I only changed the fuse.'

Walter slapped his knee and roared with laughter. 'There you are!' he said. 'Honest as the day. Marvellous boy you've got there, Barbie, one of the best. Listen,' he added to Nick, 'if I'd had to put that car into a garage they'd have stitched me up for fifty pounds *and* the rest, with some tall story about what was wrong with it. If you drive a decent car, everyone thinks you're a walking gold-mine.'

'I do *try* to be dishonest,' said Nick mildly, seeing that he was expected to be the likeable idiot. 'But I'm not very good at it.'

Everyone laughed again and Barbie said, 'What do you want to drink, love?'

'Whatever there's most of,' said Nick, and met her eye with some anxiety.

'Never you mind about that,' she said, patting his hand. 'Tim and I brought a bit extra, just in case.'

'You like Southern Comfort, don't you?' said Tim. 'With lemonade?'

'Great,' said Nick. He began to relax.

Maurice's mishap with the tea had upstaged any comment about the letters painted on the wall when Walter and Enid had come in, but their eyes kept returning to it. 'I like the decor,' said Walter. 'A timely reminder to us all. Enid will bear me out on this – I've always said, haven't I, keeping young is in the mind.'

Enid smothered a tiny yawn.

Nick was rescued by a ring at the bell. He went to the door.

'Hello, darling,' said Claudia. She had feathers in her hair and a wrap-around skirt which revealed a large expanse of fishnet-clad thigh. She pushed a bottle at him and said, 'This is Anita. You said I could bring a friend.'

The girl who was with her scowled from under a green Mohican, her eyes submerged in black mascara. She wore skin-tight black leather trousers and a lot of torn vests and chains. She stalked past Nick into the flat.

'I said, bring a *man*,' said Nick into Claudia's ear as he

84

reached past her to shut the door. She put her arm round his neck and kissed him. 'Not likely,' she murmured. 'And anyway, I'm in between men just now.'

'I admire your taste, boy,' said Walter, who had come into the hall, glass in hand. 'Got a kiss for me, too, gorgeous?'

'No,' said Claudia coldly.

Another ring turned out to be Helen and Trevor, who, as Nick had suspected, was patently dull, in a sports jacket over a yellow sweater and quietly-checked brown trousers. His hair was neatly parted on one side and he looked innocent and eager to please. Helen, however, was wearing something with layers of fringes and a long string of red beads, and looked much more striking than Nick had remembered her. She smiled at his impressed face and said, 'We meet again. It's been a long time.'

'It must be,' said Nick. She had abandoned the droopy hair-style and now had it cut short all over, brushed flat at the sides of her head and bushy on top.

'You're staring,' she said with a silver-eyelidded glance. 'Not that I mind.'

'Go on,' said Nick. 'You like it. Have a drink.' He ushered her into the living-room, where Claudia, glass in hand, was loudly demanding a felt-tip so that she could add something to what was written on the wall. Someone had turned the music up.

Anita put down an already-empty glass and turned to Nick with a rattle of chains. 'Dance,' she commanded.

'Oh, meanie,' Claudia complained, putting a possessive arm round Nick's neck. 'After all, he *is* my ex-boy friend.'

'Hang on,' said Nick. Extricating himself, he went to pour another drink.

Helen appeared at his side and he saw that Trevor had gone to sit beside Walter, apparently deep in conversation. 'What are they talking about?' he asked. 'Gas or chips?' He couldn't see that they had much else in common.

'Money,' said Helen. 'Will you dance with me?'

'Okay,' said Nick. Better than Claud and the Harrods punk, he thought. But Anita and Claudia were not so easily discarded, and Nick found himself dancing at very close quarters with three women. The doorbell rang again and he saw Maurice lurch along the hall to answer it. In the next instant, Nick found himself being surveyed with great disfavour by Sasha. Her mother stood in shocked silence beside her.

'Oh, God,' said Nick, disengaging himself with difficulty. He went over to Sasha and said, 'You got here, then.'

Sasha did not deign to reply. She was looking at Claudia with hatred.

'Have a drink,' Nick urged. 'Mrs Bowman, what would you like?'

'Joanna,' she corrected. 'Oh, I don't know. Some wine, perhaps?' She was looking from face to face nervously, and Nick remembered that her husband was supposed to be turning up tonight, for the first time in a year. Claudia was writing something on the wall with a lipstick. He glanced round for support from Barbie, but she was dancing with Tim. He poured out a glass of white wine and gave it to Joanna, desperately wondering what to do with her. He spotted Enid sitting alone, and said, 'Come and meet my aunt.'

'This is Mrs Bowman,' he said, 'Er – Joanna. This is Enid.' He found to his embarrassment that he couldn't remember Enid and Walter's surname.

'Oh, my dear, sit down,' said Enid with confidence. 'We'll watch the goings-on. Really rather quaint.'

Nick went back to Sasha. 'You look marvellous,' he said. She had gone for the full-blown film-star look, in a low-necked dress made of green taffeta, with ropes of huge imitation pearls.

'Thank you,' said Sasha coolly.

'What do you want to drink?'

'Vodka and something. I hate that girl. She was at that awful party last summer. Why did you have to ask her?'

'It was a mistake,' said Nick wearily. 'Tonic?'

'That'll do.' After a pause, and as if cross with herself for having to ask, she said, 'No news about the bike?'

'No,' said Nick. He had been trying to forget about it. Other people were arriving. Barry Winters from along the landing, with his friends Martin and Kevin and several girls, then Liz and Gary. 'Hi,' said Nick. Everyone, he saw with relief, seemed to have brought bottles.

'Any news of the bike?' asked Gary.

'No,' said Nick again. Despondency was beginning to settle over him like a fog.

Claudia sidled up to him and said, 'Introduce me to your friends, darling.'

Nick deliberately put his arm round Sasha. 'This is my girl-friend, Sasha Bowman,' he said. 'Sasha, the feathered menace here is called Claudia. General sexpot and stirrer-up of trouble.'

Claudia gave a scream of laughter. 'Darling, what a wonder-ful description!' she squealed. 'And you should know, shouldn't you!'

'My God, you've got worse,' Nick said to her, feeling Sasha stiffen.

'I have, haven't I?' said Claudia smugly. 'I've been working on it.' She stared at Sasha and added, 'Oh, I know where I've seen your little friend before. At Barry's party last year, when she got so drunk. Do you remember?'

Liz turned from the drinks table and said baldly, 'Shove off, you rotten old rat-bag.' Claudia tossed her feathered head and moved away with a mocking smile, pausing to blow a kiss at Nick.

'What an unpleasant girl,' said Joanna who, to Nick's annoy-ance, had not stayed with Enid. 'And what *are* they doing to the wall?' Cosmetic-coloured graffiti were spreading rapidly, and Kevin had just added with the spray-can he apparently carried in his pocket, LIFE IS A SEXUALLY TRANSMITTED DISEASE.

'Claud's round the twist, really,' Nick explained. 'I just thought plenty of people around would be a good thing.'

Sasha ignored him. 'Would you like a sausage on a stick?' she asked her mother.

'No, thank you,' said Joanna, still staring as if hypnotised at the wall.

'Have another drink,' Nick urged.

'Goodness, no. This'll last me for ages.' She looked as if she had found herself in a cage of baboons, Nick thought. To his relief, he saw Barbie coming back. He went to meet her and said, 'Do something about Sasha's mum before I murder her.'

'Don't be like that,' said Barbie. She greeted Joanna with a beaming smile. 'Nicky's told me such a lot about you,' she gushed. 'I'm ever so glad we've met at last. You play the piano, don't you? You'd laugh, you know, we've got an old boy plays the piano in the bar, Saturday nights, talk about terrible! Bennie Eggitt, his name is, fancies himself a real little Liberace.' Nick gave her a grateful nod. It was amazing he thought, how she could turn on a tide of easy talk. No wonder she was good at running a pub.

Sasha was nursing an empty glass and she looked at Nick accusingly as he took it from her to refill. 'Why did you have to ask that girl?' she demanded. 'And don't give me that stuff about it being a mistake.'

Nick shrugged, pouring her another drink. 'I just pulled up at traffic lights one day, and there she was in a sports car,' he said. 'So I thought – '

'Yes, she would have a sports car, wouldn't she,' said Sasha bitterly. 'She's the one with a rich father.'

'That's not my fault,' Nick objected. To his irritation, he could see Maurice making his way towards them, glass in hand.

'Hello,' said Maurice genially. 'Are you having a good time?'

'Yes, thank you, Mr Cartwright,' said Sasha, with a hostile glance at Nick.

'You know,' said Maurice sentimentally, with his head on one side, 'you remind me of a girl I met in Germany, when I was in the Army. Helga. Lovely girl she was. Curly hair like yours, blue eyes – I really fancied her. Thing was, though, she'd only got one leg.'

Nick gave a snort of laughter and Sasha collapsed into giggles.

'No, straight up,' Maurice protested. 'If it hadn't been for that, you might have fetched up with her for a mother, Nick, instead of the old battle-axe over there.'

'Mum's all right,' said Nick, noticing that Joanna Bowman,

in conversation with Barbie, was smiling for once in her life. 'Look at all this spread she's laid on.'

'Oh, stick up for her, yes, that's you all over,' said Maurice. He tapped himself in the chest and added, 'Who thought of it, eh? It's the planning that counts, boy. A general doesn't go out and dig the latrines, does he? No, he gets the squaddies to do that. Strategy, that's what counts. That's his job.' He was very drunk again.

'I'm sure it does,' said Sasha, putting her glass down. 'Nick, let's go and dance.'

'Call that dancing!' Maurice shouted after them. 'Not like we used to do it. I could show you something!' Then, as more people came in, 'Terry! Come on in, mate. You're just in time, before these buggers drink it all.'

For once, Nick thought, his father had done him a favour, albeit unknowingly. Once Sasha had laughed, she could never recapture a cross mood. 'Isn't it weird,' she said in his ear. 'There's several different parties all going on at once in this room. It's such a crazy assortment of people. Each lot is having quite a different experience.'

Nick shrugged. He didn't want to theorise about it. He saw Paul with Phil and Roger from Greenwich. 'Come and meet these guys,' he said. 'They're okay.'

Towing Sasha by the hand, he started across the room. Enid was having a shouted conversation about hotel carpeting with Tim, and Trevor was now being danced with by an energetic West Indian girl whose beaded dreadlocks occasionally flicked him in the face. Joanna, he saw, had got drawn into Maurice's group, where a curly-haired tarmac-layer called Alec stood gazing at her respectfully, glass raised. 'You're a handsome woman, my dear,' he was assuring her. 'An ex-cep-tionally handsome woman.' Maurice's friends seemed to be permanently blotto, Nick thought. Still, Joanna seemed to like it. She was smiling quite radiantly.

'Freshen you up?' offered Walter when Nick and Sasha reached the drinks table. He seemed to have taken it on himself to play the role of host, since nobody was talking to him much, probably because he was quite exceptionally boring.

Walter looked at Sasha appreciatively and said, 'Another pretty girl! My word, you do pick 'em, Nick!' All the delicacy of a bulldozer, Nick thought. But Walter went on, 'You're David Bowman's girl, aren't you. Seen your face in the Abrahams' catalogue. I know Joss and Myra very well.'

'*Do* you?' said Sasha eagerly. 'Aren't they darlings! Have you met Bernie?'

Nick left them in animated conversation. Paul and the others had eluded him, and were adding to the increasingly elaborate decoration of the wall. He wondered whether to join them, and decided he couldn't be bothered. It was all going better than he had dared to hope for, and people seemed to be enjoying themselves, but he couldn't feel part of it. Time was dragging.

The evening wore on slowly. People drank and danced, picked at the food and added more and more bits of writing to the scrawled-over wall. Maurice sat on a chair, staring at everyone with eyes that glared from his red face, but his friends surrounded him like a kind of noisy, cheerful padding, so far preventing his fury from boiling over. Sasha was dancing with Roger. Nick felt a kind of aching numbness. He wished he could be part of the general enjoyment, but all he wanted was to be on his own somewhere.

He went into the bathroom and used the toilet, then washed his hands slowly, sitting on the edge of the bath to dry them until someone rattled at the door to come in. Enid was waiting outside when he emerged. 'Thank you,' she said crisply. Nick wondered if he should go back and polish the seat. He picked up his glass from where he had parked it in the hall and stood with it in his hand. He felt very, very sober. He opened the front door and went out on to the glassed-in balcony, and walked along to where one of the sliding windows stood open. There, he leaned his elbows on the window's edge, his glass cradled between his hands, and stared out.

Thousands of lights studded the dark landscape. Thousands of people, he thought, all doing whatever it was they happened to be engaged in, and to each one of them it was as real and immediate as the pressure of his arms on the window ledge was to him, here and now. As Sasha had said, everyone was having their own particular experience. He didn't know what was real to anyone else, and they didn't know what was real to him. Everyone was alone. The pointlessness of it all was overwhelming and somehow terribly sad. And yet, he thought, there could not be any point. If there was one simple purpose, it would turn life into a giant conveyor belt. It would be intolerable.

Nick tensed slightly as he became aware that someone was pushing open the door at the end of the balcony. The instinct to turn and face a stranger was very strong, but Nick did not want the involvement which meeting the eye of another human being would imply. He was a part of the dark air which separated him from the distant lights. He was nothing.

The man who had come along the balcony paused by the open door of the flat from which the sound of the party came pouring out, and Nick felt himself being surveyed. He kept completely still, but the man approached him and stopped.

'It is Nick Cartwright, isn't it?' he said.

Reluctantly, Nick turned round. He found himself face to face with Sasha's father.

Chapter 10

David Bowman had wiry grey hair which stuck up like a well-clipped hedge from round his bald patch. He looked thinner, Nick thought, than when he had last seen him, several months ago. And slightly younger.

'Have you come out for a breath of fresh air?' David asked, joining Nick at the window.

'Something like that.'

After a pause, David said, 'To be honest, I don't much like parties.'

Nick did not answer. I bet you don't like this one, he thought. Meeting the wife you'd left a year ago wouldn't be a lot of fun.

91

'You seem a bit depressed,' David ventured.

Nick wondered if depression was the right word for what he felt, and nodded. It was near enough. 'A bit,' he said.

'It's funny how these occasions so often have that effect,' David went on. 'It's all supposed to be wildly special, but when it comes to the point, you're still living with the same old self.'

'Yeah,' agreed Nick. 'That's it.'

After another pause, David took an untidy package from under his arm and said, 'I didn't wrap this up, I'm afraid.'

Nick took the brown paper bag and looked inside. 'A road atlas!' he said. 'Hey – two road atlases! Britain and Europe. Thanks a lot.'

'I thought hard-backed ones would stand up to a bit of use,' said David. 'I didn't know what you wanted, but they always come in handy when you're planning a journey. Have bike, will travel.'

'Haven't bike,' said Nick. 'The bloody thing was pinched this morning. But thanks all the same.'

'Oh, no!' David seemed genuinely concerned. 'That's awful. The thought of someone else on *your* bike – '

'Makes you sick,' said Nick.

'I had a Norton,' said David, 'years ago. I sold it, though, when I got married. Joanna didn't fancy riding pillion.'

Nick smiled briefly and said, 'No.'

'Is she in there?' asked David, nodding at the doorway of the flat.

'Yes,' said Nick. 'And Sasha. I suppose we'd better go in.'

David hesitated. 'How is she?' he asked.

'She's had her hair done,' said Nick evasively. It was a question he couldn't answer. 'She looks – different.'

David waited for more.

'She's going to play the piano for a ballet class.' Nick gave up. 'I don't know how she is,' he said. 'She sighs a lot. But she always did.'

David stared out at the distant estate, looking at the pattern of lights. 'All pretty tense, I expect,' he said.

'No,' said Nick. 'She's being chatted up by one of my dad's mates from the pub.'

David laughed and said, 'Marvellous.' He thought for a minute, then made a decision. 'I hope you'll forgive me,' he said, 'but I don't think I'm going to come in.'

'You can't do that,' said Nick promptly. 'It would be a let-down.'

David seemed confused. 'I don't want to cause any sort of upset,' he explained.

'You won't,' Nick promised rashly. 'You don't have to stick around for long − just have a drink then shove off again. I mean − you'll have to meet her sooner or later. And she's all psyched up to it.'

David nodded slowly and said, 'You're perfectly right. I suppose I'm just being a coward.'

Nick remembered what Sasha had said about her father showing nothing but the acceptable side of his personality for so many years, and smiled inwardly. Yes, this meeting must be the last thing he wanted. 'Go on,' he said. 'It'll be all right.' Mentally, he crossed his fingers.

The flat was now in almost total darkness as most of the lights had been turned out, and the hot, noisy essence of the party came out to meet them like a gale of used air blowing from a subway ventilator. Screams of laughter came from the deco-rated wall, where Barry was holding up some girl so that she could add a scrawled obscenity at ceiling level to the crammed and intricate graffiti. Nick saw that Sasha was having an earnest conversation with Roger near the kitchen door. The music was deafening. 'What would you like to drink?' he shouted to David over his shoulder.

'Whisky?' David shouted back.

The drinks table looked seriously depleted, and Barbie was dancing with Walter. Nick found Tim and said, 'Is there any whisky? Sasha's father's just arrived.'

'Special reserve,' said Tim, reaching into a carrier bag under the table.

Nick could at first see no sign of Joanna, then she came past in the arms of Alec, dancing in a swooping ballroom style to the thumping Heavy Metal beat. 'A lovely dancer, is Alec,' remarked Maurice, who was propped against the sideboard, a hand clamped round his glass as if it was part of him. 'Lovely.'

David's eyes followed his wife as he tasted his drink. She was smiling girlishly, tra-la-la-ing to the music. As Alec steered her into a flashy turn, she saw David, and for a moment her eyes widened. David raised a hand, and she waved back, then went on dancing.

'There you are,' said Nick. 'Easy.'

'That much, yes,' said David.

Sasha came over and beamed at her father, kissing him. 'I'm so glad you've come,' she said. 'I thought you were going to chicken out.'

'I nearly did,' said her father. 'You've got Nick to thank for talking me into it.'

Sasha tucked her arm into Nick's and said, 'Aren't you clever!' Nick felt relieved. After the Claud incident, he needed to get his stripes back.

The record ended and Joanna made her way towards them, patting at her hair nervously.

'Hello, Jo,' said her husband. 'How are you?'

'Fine,' she said defiantly. 'Just fine.' She turned to Nick with unusual gaiety. 'What a lovely party,' she said. 'I do think it was a brilliant idea, letting everyone do a mural. They're really enjoying it.'

'I like your hair,' said David cautiously. 'Very smart. Can I get you a drink?'

'Thank you,' said Joanna.

Cross-eyed Terry stopped beside her and said, 'Hello, there.' He was weaving slightly. 'Haven't I met you before?' he ventured. 'Were you here last night when we all came back from the pub? Now, *that* was a party, wasn't it!'

Nick smiled to himself. So both he and Maurice had celebrated this birthday on the previous night. No wonder everything seemed so insignificant now.

Joanna looked at Terry with queenly dignity and said, 'No, this is the first time we have met.'

'Ah, but we're old friends in the spirit,' said Terry sentimentally. 'Old friends.'

Maurice lurched up, clasping a party can of beer in his free arm, the other still grasping his glass, and shouted obscurely, 'Come on, now, let's be having you!' The Army, Nick thought, had a lot to answer for.

At this moment, Tim banged loudly on the table and shouted, 'Ladies and gentlemen, a bit of hush, if you please!'

'What's he on about?' Maurice grumbled.

'No birthday is complete without a cake,' Tim went on over the slightly reduced noise. 'And that goes for this one, too! Bring it in, Barbie!'

Nick's mother came in, her face lit by a blaze of radiance from the candle-lit cake she carried into the dark room. Everyone clapped and cheered. Nick felt as if he was watching a re-run film. He caught Liz's eye and leaned across to say, 'Your bike one was better.' But some superstitious part of his mind nagged at him with mocking insistence. He had enjoyed himself too much at that other party. There was no bike now, 'Where's Gary?' he asked, pushing the thought away.

'Throwing up, I expect,' said Liz cheerfully. 'You know what he's like. At least I only do it in the mornings!'

'It must be awful,' said Nick. 'Don't you ever wish you hadn't got pregnant?'

'No,' said Liz serenely. 'It'll be worth it. Go on, you'll have to blow the candles out.'

Everyone was shouting for Nick. What a prat, he thought. What a complete narna. He approached the table and looked down at the mass of burning candles whose heat rose in his face. He gathered a huge breath, and blew. A few small flames remained, and he blew again. Gone. Just wisps of smoke and faintly-glowing wicks. And all the idiots cheering.

'You might look a bit happy about it,' said Maurice at his side. Nick glanced at his father and saw in the puffy eyes a cold, dispassionate understanding. For a chilling moment, he and his father looked at each other as if they were alone in an empty room, then Nick turned his head away to avoid the nakedness of that gaze. Was that why Maurice drank? To fend off that implacable, unbearable knowledge of the way things were? 'Smile,' said Maurice. 'Bloody smile.' He tipped some beer untidily from the party can into his glass, and the moment of communication was over.

A knife was being put into Nick's hands. 'Just make one cut, love,' Barbie instructed from his other side. 'Tim and I will portion it up.'

So here he stood, Nick thought, between his parents, receiving the benefit of their combined advice, for the first time in years. He pushed the knife down through the hard white icing.

'Speech!' shouted Walter, and Gary, white-faced but enthusiastic, called, 'Come on, Nick! Say a few words!'

Feet were stamped, tables thumped. Oh, shit, thought Nick desperately. What did people say on these occasions? Thanked their mothers and fathers, he supposed. For the sexually-transmitted gift of life. A playground rhyme came back to his mind and he heard himself saying it aloud.

'God bless Mum and God bless Dad.

They're both bloody nuts, but they're all I had.'

Everyone cheered and whistled ironically. Sasha kissed him and David said, 'Well done.'

'Not really,' said Nick dispassionately.

Liz looked at him and asked, 'You all right, Nick? You seem a bit – off.'

'Yeah,' said Nick. 'Just a bit.'

Liz tried to cheer him up, but he let her voice blend in with the thumping music and made no effort to understand what she was saying. After a bit she gave him a last encouraging smile and went off to dance with Gary.

The party went on, and Nick watched it. Sasha, he noticed, sat and talked in a smiling shout to her parents for a bit, then got up to dance with Paul. Terry approached Joanna with an old-fashioned and slightly unsteady bow, inviting her to dance, and David waved his assent. He stood up as his wife waltzed away with Terry, and made his way towards Nick at the door. 'I think I'll be off,' he said.

Nick went out with him. On the balcony, David turned and looked at him. 'What are you going to do, Nick?' he asked.

'Good question,' said Nick.

'If I can help in any way – ' David said tentatively. 'Not that you'd think of going into banking, I suppose, but I do meet people from time to time who are looking for a bright young man to start. It's not so much educational qualifications as someone who knows how to think on his feet. You know what I mean?'

'Thanks,' said Nick. It must be a big effort, he thought, for a man like David to see a leather-jacketed yob as a bright young man. Nice of him to try. But nine-to-five, in a natty suit? Promotion like a pat on the head if you were enough of a creep? Ludicrous. 'I don't know,' he said, not wanting to sound ungrateful. 'Things are a bit of a mess.'

'They'll work out, one way or another,' said David. 'They always do. Keep in touch. Say good-bye to Sasha for me. I'll see her soon. Both of you, I hope. So long.'

'See you,' said Nick. Then he went back into the flat.

Maurice met him at the door, looking aggrieved. 'What the hell are they smoking in there?' he demanded. 'It smells like old carpets.'

'What d'you *think* they're smoking?' asked Nick, who had seen Barry rolling his first joint hours ago.

'I'm not having this place used for taking drugs!' Maurice protested. His face was very red and he was sweating profusely.

'Oh, don't be stupid,' said Nick. 'You don't mind people getting out of their heads on alcohol.'

'Thass different,' said Maurice doggedly.

'No, it isn't,' Nick argued, suddenly angry because of the bleakness of his evening. 'Alcohol's a drug. You don't *think*, do you? You just reckon booze is okay because everyone does it. A night out with the boys, ho-ho, and never mind if you're wrecked in the morning. Look at you now, you can hardly stand up. People don't get like that on pot.'

Maurice pointed an unsteady finger at him and said, 'You've tried it, haven't you. You're a bloody drug addict.'

Nick looked at him with contempt. 'If anyone's a drug addict round here, it's you,' he said, and pushed past his father into the dark living-room.

Maurice, at the door, switched the light on. There were shouts of protest. In the sudden, hard light, the room looked astonishingly squalid. 'I'm not having the place used for drug orgies!' shouted Maurice. 'What do you think this is? I'm not – '

Barbie reached past him and switched the light off again. A violent altercation broke out at once. Nick could hear his father shouting abuse at Barbie, and Tim's voice sounding strident as he tried to pacify the enraged man. His intervention made things worse, and Nick heard Walter say, 'Now, Morrie, let's not spoil the party, eh?'

'Party?' yelled Maurice. 'Whose fucking party is this, anyway? Who's the off – ' he spluttered and tried again, thumping himself in the chest, 'Officer-in-charge? I am!'

In the brief moment when the light was on, Nick had seen Helen sitting on a chair by the window with her hands in her lap. She looked as if she was the one person in the room who was enjoying the party less than Nick was. He made his way across to her and squatted down beside her chair. 'What's the matter?' he asked.

She shook her head blindly.

'Where's Trevor-of-the-Gas-Board?' asked Nick.

After a few moments, Helen blurted, 'I could kill that girl.'

'Which one?' asked Nick, although he knew who Helen must mean. Asking Claud here had been like putting a vulture in a cage of budgies.

'That one with the feathers. I was talking to some other people for a bit, and I saw her dancing with Trevor, and now they've both disappeared. I think she's taken him home with her. They're not in the flat. I've looked everywhere.'

Maurice switched the light on again and Walter shouted something at him and switched it off.

'There's going to be an awful row,' said Nick.

'I want to go home,' said Helen. 'I hate this party.'

'That makes two of us,' said Nick. 'How did you get here?'

'With Trevor,' said Helen wretchedly. 'In his car. I feel such a fool.'

'If you've got the keys, I should take it and go,' said Nick. 'To hell with him. Claud's probably kidnapped him in the X 19.' He laughed at the thought of natty little Trevor in

Claudia's clutches, and Helen looked at him doubtfully. 'Him and Claud,' said Nick. 'It's like a guinea pig in bed with a tiger. He'll get claud to death.' It was a joke from years back, but Helen laughed guiltily. 'That's vile,' she said. 'And I haven't got the keys, anyway.' She relapsed into misery. 'He's probably taken his car. And even if he hasn't, I can't drive. I'm learning, but I haven't passed my test yet.'

'A man has rights!' Maurice was shouting. 'In his own house!' He was surrounded by a crowd of people trying to pacify him. The music was still playing loudly. Sasha was dancing with Roger again, Nick noticed. He had a strong feeling of being in the dog-house.

Liz appeared with a glass of lemonade in her hand and, shouting to make herself heard, said, 'Funny not drinking. I've gone right off it. Makes you feel out of things, though.'

Nick nodded. She wasn't the only one.

'The Bowman get-together was a success,' Liz went on. 'Mrs B's gone home, but she's okay. Said would I say good-night to you for her.'

'Right,' said Nick. Thank God for that, he thought. The lights went on and off again. This was getting ridiculous.

'I want to go home,' said Helen again.

Nick looked at her with faint irritation. He would have to do something about her. He wondered if Anita would know whose car Claud had taken. 'Back in a minute,' he said, and pushed his way through the crowded room until he found Anita, who had started scrawling on a new wall.

'Where's Claud?' he enquired.

'Gone home,' said Anita laconically.

'In her car?'

Anita looked at him disparagingly and said, 'Well, she wasn't going to walk, was she?'

Nick thought quickly. Anita had arrived with Claud, most probably in her car. And she seemed suspiciously unconcerned about not having a lift home.

'That's a downer, isn't it?' he said innocently. 'She's left you with no transport.'

Anita gave a faint sneer which he interpreted as a smile. 'Got the keys of little Boy-wonder's car, haven't I?' she said. 'Fair swop. He was too pissed to drive, anyway.'

Nick held out his hand. 'Come on,' he said. 'I've got to take his girl friend home. Claud's mucked her up good and proper.'

'No,' said Anita. 'I'm not getting stuck here all night.'

'I won't *be* all night,' said Nick, exasperated. Under the green hair, Anita's face was petulant, and he realised that she wasn't enjoying this party, either. Understandably, nobody liked her much. He managed to smile at her. 'I'll be back,' he said earnestly.

'Yeah?' With some difficulty, she managed to wriggle her fingers into the pocket of her skin-tight leather trousers. She dropped the keys into his hand and looked him up and down speculatively. 'The blokes here are a load of wets,' she said.

'I'll be back,' Nick promised, and beat a hasty retreat.

Helen had not moved, and Liz was perched protectively on the arm of her chair. 'I reckon we're in for a fight,' she said, looking at the arguing group by the door, which had been joined by all Maurice's friends. 'You were never fit to be a father!' Barbie was shouting.

Just like old times, Nick thought. 'Come on,' he said to Helen. If there was going to be a scene, he'd rather be somewhere else. She stood up, and he led her towards the door. Anyway, he thought, it would be interesting to see what sort of car Trevor Gasboard drove. 'Tell Sasha I'll be back soon!' he called to Liz, who raised a casual thumb, and continued her way through the crowd in search of Gary.

The car turned out to be an Alfasud. Much too good for its owner, Nick thought as he started it up. These were quite sporty. He drove it gently out into the main road and turned right as instructed by Helen, resisting the temptation to thrash it. He had probably drunk enough to turn a bag green, though he still felt dismally sober. Helen sat silently beside him as he headed for Lewisham.

'You turn left after the swimming baths,' she said eventually, and then gave efficient instructions until he pulled up outside a tall Victorian house.

'Socking great place,' he said, peering out at it.

'It's divided into flats,' said Helen. 'I share the top one with two other girls.' After a pause, she added, 'I shall never see Trevor again, you know.'

'Don't blame you,' said Nick. He wished she would hurry up and get out.

'Would you like to come in for some coffee?' asked Helen.

'No, thanks,' Nick said firmly. She must be joking. He wasn't kidnap material. Not tonight, anyway. Not with Sasha still at the party, even if she was trying to make him jealous, dancing with Roger all the time.

'You must have thought I was awfully tarty,' said Helen suddenly.

'Must I?' asked Nick. He wondered what she was talking about.

'I always wanted you to notice me,' Helen confessed. 'When I was just a schoolgirl, after Dad first got to know your mother, you used to be around with marvellous-looking girl friends, and I felt as if I was nothing at all.'

'You were something tonight all right,' said Nick. 'In all those fringes.' He was looking forward to driving the car on his own, without the inhibition of a passenger.

'Really?' She looked up at him, and in the next minute he found that he was kissing her. Damn, he thought. He had not planned this. He ought to go back to the party in case Maurice was causing havoc. But then, he thought, relaxing, it would only make things worse if he went and put his oar in.

It was some time before Helen got out of the car. Feeling sorry for people was awful, Nick thought guiltily as she turned at the gate to smile and wave. It made it seem as if you were doing things out of duty. He waved back, cheerily, and drove off up the road.

He found himself in a maze of tree-lined streets, expecting at any minute to hit the one-way system which would lead him back on to Lewisham Way, but instead, he found himself not far from Blackheath. What the heck, he thought. He would go down Shooters Hill and into New Cross that way, then back up the Old Kent Road. It wasn't much further.

In another half-mile, the Alfa's engine suddenly faltered. It recovered, coughed a couple of times and then died. Nick coasted round the corner into a side street, cursing. There was unlikely to be a tool kit in the car. Trevor wouldn't know a spanner from a nail file. He stopped under a street light and investigated, discovering the simple truth that the car was out of petrol.

He couldn't believe it. Had the idiot really driven to a party with barely half a pint in the tank? Or had he simply neglected to lock the petrol cap? That was asking to get the stuff siphoned out. Nick locked the car and walked away from it nonchalantly, trying to look as if he had merely parked it.

What on earth was the time? It must be at least half-past one, if not later. Bloody marvellous, Nick thought. Marooned in sodding Blackheath in the middle of the night, with no money on him. He hadn't even got a jacket. He had come out of the flat exactly as he was, still wearing the shirt he had borrowed from Gary earlier today. Yesterday, he corrected himself. This was now Monday morning. And his twenty-first birthday was, thank God, over.

Chapter 11

Nick stood on the pavement's edge and waited. There was not much traffic about, but after a while a big Scania lorry came into sight and he stuck out his thumb hopefully. The lorry pulled up with a hiss of air brakes and Nick put his foot in the step beside the front wheel and heaved himself up to open the door. 'Are you going through the Elephant?' he asked.

'Aye. Get in,' said the driver.

Nick climbed in and pulled the door shut, and the lorry moved off. 'Where are you heading for?' he asked.

'Aberdeen.' The driver seemed to be a man of few words.

Nick nodded casually, but the thought of going to Aberdeen in this huge vehicle was a curiously intriguing one. He toyed with the idea of asking if he could come all the way. The Scania's cab was comfortable and warm, with the radio playing and a couple of plastic flowers stuck in a holder on the dash and a sticker saying, 'A1 Truckers' Club' pasted across the top of the windscreen. Home, sweet home, he thought. Long-distance driving would be a pretty good job. He remembered the road atlases David had given him and wondered with renewed gloom whether he would ever use them.

He got out of the lorry at the red traffic lights just short of the Elephant roundabout, and walked back through the estate to the flat. As he emerged from the lift, he could hear music playing, but it was from somewhere along the other balcony, where Barry lived. He let himself in through his front door.

Sasha came to meet him, but she stopped short of him, arms folded.

'The car ran out of petrol,' he said. 'Honest. I've had to hitch back.'

She glanced at him tiredly and did not answer. It looked bad, he realised. He had disappeared for hours with the girl Sasha had seen him dancing with earlier on. Sasha turned to go back into the living-room, but he caught her arm and said, 'Hang on. Sasha, don't be cross. Please. There's been enough aggro tonight.'

'You can say that again,' she said.

He pulled her to him and kissed her, and she gave a shaky sigh. 'You really are dreadful,' she said.

'Funny, isn't it,' said Nick, thinking about the inevitability of his dreadfulness. 'It just seems to happen.'

Sasha looked up at him. 'Sometimes I just feel I can't cope,' she said. 'This evening's been absolutely awful.'

Nick refrained from saying that she appeared to have been having quite a good time with Roger. Instead, he said, 'The old man threw a mental, did he?'

'*Did* he,' said Sasha with feeling. 'Thank goodness my mother went home, that's all. I don't know *what* she'd have thought.' She released herself from Nick's embrace and he followed her back into the debris-littered room, where Liz was curled up on the sofa with her head on Gary's shoulder. The

103

only other person present was Anita, who scowled from an arm chair, one leather-clad leg slung over its arm. 'About bloody time,' she said. 'You've got a funny idea of coming straight back. Such a dull-looking girl, too.'

'Listen, you muck-raking old bag,' said Nick, 'I've had to hitch back from Blackheath. The car's out of petrol.'

'Black*heath*!' squawked Anita. 'What the hell's it doing at Blackheath? That's miles away! How am I going to get home?'

'Broomstick?' Liz suggested sweetly.

Anita ignored her. 'For God's sake,' she raged. 'I've only been hanging on in this dump for Trevor's car.'

'There's all-night buses every half-hour,' said Gary.

Anita glared at him. 'If you think I'm walking to a bus stop through this awful estate, dressed like this,' she said, 'you've got to be joking.'

Everyone laughed. 'Scared you might meet a punk?' Liz suggested. 'A real one?'

'Oh, get stuffed,' snarled Anita, and uncurled herself from the chair. 'I suppose I'll have to ring for a taxi.'

When Anita had taken herself off, Nick and Sasha and Gary and Liz sat and looked at each other in silence. The room, with its spent-party smell of ash and pastry and assorted booze, seemed squalid and exhausted.

'Is the old man in bed?' asked Nick.

'No,' said Sasha. 'Those friends of his took him somewhere with them. I was glad they did. I thought someone was going to get badly hurt.'

Liz got up and went into the kitchen, where Nick heard the tap running and crockery being clattered. 'Don't start washing up, Liz!' he called.

'I'm not!' Liz shouted back. 'Just four mugs so we can have some coffee.'

Gary put on an old Santana record and Sasha went on with her account of what had happened since Nick left the flat. He listened unwillingly. It was all so predictable – Maurice's increasingly furious tirade about pot-smoking and the wall and Young People Today, and Barbie's inevitable loss of temper.

There was no half-way with her. She flared up violently and without warning.

'The trouble was Tim, really,' said Gary. 'You could see he thought Barbie was going to get flattened at any minute, so he did his heavy landlord act. "Behave yourself now, Maurice. We don't want any unpleasantness." '

Nick groaned and put his hand over his face. That would be the end.

'So Maurice took a swing at him with a bottle,' Gary went on. 'And there was quite a brawl. The people from next door came in, complaining about the noise, and so did the people who live underneath. They said they were going to get the police.'

'That curly-haired man called Alec just bundled Maurice out when they said that,' Sasha put in, 'and the others all went with him. Your Auntie Enid said it was the most disgusting thing she'd ever seen, and her husband kept shouting at everyone. And Tim was absolutely furious. Once Maurice had gone, Barbie got over her temper and said she wanted to stay and do the clearing up, but Tim wouldn't hear of it. He was awfully cross because you'd disappeared, Nick. He called you an ungrateful hound.'

'You can see how he felt,' remarked Liz, coming in with two mugs of coffee in each hand. 'They'll have had to pay stand-in help to look after the pub, and they'd done a big job with the food and supplied a lot of booze as well, and what for? The host gets into a drunken brawl and Birthday Boy shoves off in someone else's car, with someone else's girl friend. Who happens to be Tim's daughter,' she added, then grinned. 'So a jolly good time was had by all.'

'It's still going on at Barry's place,' said Sasha.

Gary prodded Liz gently and said, 'You realise we've got to be on the plane at twenty to eight in the morning?'

'Hardly worth going to bed,' said Liz. 'But we can sleep all the way to Sweden. Let's do the washing up. If we all give a hand it won't take long.'

'No,' said Nick.

Liz began to argue, but he held up a lordly hand. 'You two

are off on holiday,' he pointed out, 'and Sasha's going to work, and I'm going nowhere. I'll do the washing up. I can take all day over it if I like. All week. I'm unemployed, remember?'

'Great,' said Gary. 'It's all yours, mate.'

Thanks a lot, thought Nick. He didn't have to accept the offer with quite such alacrity.

He set about the clearing up as soon as the others had gone. It would seem worse in the morning, and Maurice would start another tirade if he came back and found the flat in this state.

By the time Nick had finished, daylight was breaking. He pulled the curtains back and looked out at the city, quiet in the grey, early light. Somewhere, in that network of streets and buildings, he had to find a job, he supposed. The business of living had to be continued. The ants in the ant-heap, of which he was one, had to keep scurrying on in the appointed pattern. It was a profoundly wearying prospect. Nick turned away from the window and went into his bedroom, where the closed, green-patterned curtains still excluded the light. He took off his clothes and went to bed.

He woke to the sound of the telephone ringing. He burrowed back into the dream. There was some great waterway running down the place where Wandsworth High Street used to be, and a wavering bridge over it, hardly wide enough for the bike he was riding . . . .

Maurice banged on the door and shouted, 'It's that girl of yours.'

The water was rushing past below him. He was in a hurry, with his big parcel strapped to his back. He had always meant to get a carrier . . . .

'You dead or something?' bawled Maurice.

Nick did not want to open his eyes. It would shatter the dream, drop him back into reality which he did not want to know. His father came into the room and shook him by the shoulder.

'Sod off,' muttered Nick.

'Suit yourself,' said Maurice, and retreated. Nick heard him

106

say, 'Can't get no sense out of him. You best ring later on.'

The dream was slipping away. In its place, Nick knew, was the familiar room with its cream-painted walls and the patches of bare plaster where he had sellotaped posters up when he had been interested in the pops. A pile of clothes back from the launderette would be lying on the chest of drawers with a copy of *Superbike* and an ashtray. Nothing to wake up for. But a remorseless tension had crept into his limbs and the comfort of sleep was ebbing, together with the other world of his dreaming. He lay inert, trying to coax his dream back, but the doors to unreality seemed closed now, and he could not find the way to let his mind slip out into fantasy's escape. He lay for a long time in the nothingness between the two worlds, and a clammy stillness settled over him, stone-like and unrewarding behind the darkness of his closed eyelids, but better than the cream walls and the ashtray.

The telephone rang again.

'Oh, bloody 'ell,' he heard Maurice grumble. 'You don't give up, do you? Hang on. NICK!' he yelled. 'Chrissake come and talk to this girl, will you?'

Nick found himself getting out of bed. Outside the curtains it was dark again. He pulled on his underpants and went out to the telephone. He felt stone-like and remote. 'Hi,' he said.

'Oh, Nick,' said Sasha. 'I've been thinking about you all day. Why didn't you answer the phone? Are you all right?'

Nick considered this. Would she think he was all right? This sense of remoteness had been bad at the party, but it was worse now.

'Nick?' She sounded anxious. 'What's the matter?'

'Dunno,' said Nick. 'Nothing.' Nothing matters, he thought. That was it, really. There was no point.

'No word of the bike?'

'No.' It was a terribly empty word.

'Don't get depressed about it,' Sasha urged. 'You'll get the insurance money. And couldn't you buy some old banger meanwhile and do it up?'

In a twelfth-floor flat? Nick thought wearily. Oh, great. And Gary had gone off to Sweden. He couldn't even work on

107

something in that little shed of his.

'Nick? Do *talk* to me. Look, it'll be all right. You'll find another job and get another bike. Things'll work out.'

'Yeah,' said Nick. Then off we go again, he thought, same old pattern, work at something boring all day so as to get just enough money at the end of the week to pay Maurice for a share of this grotty flat, run the bike, take Sasha out once or twice. Was that what she meant by all right? There was a draught blowing in from the hall and his bare feet were getting cold. Sasha was still saying a lot of hopeful things and he waited for her to pause. Then he said, 'See you tomorrow, right?' It was an automatic signing-off line. He added, 'Dunno how, though.' He didn't much care.

'I'll come round,' said Sasha firmly. 'Straight from work. You will be there, won't you?'

Nick almost laughed, but not quite. How would he be anywhere else? 'Yeah,' he said. 'I'll be here.' Then he replaced the receiver and went back to bed.

The night seemed endlessly long, but Nick, lying open-eyed in the dark, was in no hurry for the daylight. There was no purpose for him in its arrival. Outside this private nest of a bed was nothing but boredom and impossibility. It was all pointless. He fell asleep a little before dawn and managed to ignore a minor outburst of abuse from Maurice at twenty-past seven. At two o'clock that afternoon he got up for a pee and ate some cold baked beans out of a tin. He looked at the sitting-room walls and their plastered graffiti, and felt invaded. It was as if the street had marched in. He drank half a cup of tea, lost interest in it, and went back to bed.

Some hours later, Maurice slammed the front door behind him. A few minutes later, he came into Nick's room. 'What d'you think you're doing?' he demanded.

'Nothing,' said Nick with truth. He lay as still as a stone.

'What d'you mean, nothing? You can get this bloody living-room painted, to start with. Then get your arse down the DHSS and sign on.'

Nick did not answer. There was no point. If he kept his eyes shut for long enough, everything would stop happening.

'I'm not having this staying-in-bed business,' said Maurice. He stepped forward and snatched the bedclothes off. Naked, Nick grabbed at his coverings and yelled, 'Fuck off!'

For a moment, there was an absurd tug-of-war with the sheet, then the doorbell rang. Maurice did not let go. 'One of your bloody friends,' he said.

'Well, answer it, then!' shouted Nick, and snatched the sheet from his father's grasp.

'*You* answer it!' snapped Maurice. With a quick heave, he jerked both blankets clear of the mattress and quickly left the room with them.

Cursing, Nick draped himself in the sheet and went to the door as the bell rang again.

'Nick,' said Sasha. 'What on earth's going on?'

Nick stumped back to his bedroom without answering. Sasha closed the front door and followed him, sitting down on the edge of the blanketless bed beside him.

'Go on then,' said Nick after a few moments' silence.

'Go on what?'

'Say your little piece. Tell me I ought to pull myself together.'

Sasha regarded him steadily then said, 'Would you like a cup of tea?'

Nick, huddled under his sheet, shrugged his shoulders.

'I'll go and make one,' said Sasha.

He heard her arguing briskly with Maurice in the kitchen, and reached for his underpants.

When he got into the kitchen a few minutes later, Maurice was prodding irritably at some sausages in a frying pan while Sasha stood beside the kettle with her arms folded. But at least they were both quiet, Nick thought. He went back into the living-room and picked up his blankets from the chair where Maurice had thrown them. Maurice came out and said, 'I don't want your women in my kitchen.'

'She's not women,' said Nick. 'There's only one of her.'

'Without a by-your-leave,' said Maurice. 'Just bloody walk in.'

'Oh, shut up,' said Nick, and carried the blankets back to his room, where he draped them over himself, huddled like a Red Indian on the pillow at the top of his bed. Sasha came in with two mugs of tea. This time she sat on the chair beside the garment-littered chest of drawers, as if she was a Health Visitor, Nick thought. There was a long silence while they sipped their tea, looked at each other, and looked away. The smell of Maurice's sausages drifted from the kitchen and Nick found with vague annoyance that he was hungry.

'I've been thinking,' said Sasha.

He did not answer. Hunger and irritation were prodding him out of his immobility, and he resented it. Sasha, too, was a disturber. Why was it so difficult to be left alone?

'I know everything's dreadful at the moment,' Sasha went on, 'and I know you just want to lie there and die, but honestly, things don't happen for no purpose.'

'Spare me the crud,' said Nick.

Sasha banged her mug of tea down on the chest of drawers and jumped to her feet. 'You know what?' she accused him. 'You are just *feeble*. When you get these misery moods, you don't even try to get out of them. You just let them sprawl over you, and over anyone who has anything to do with you, until we're *all* miserable.'

If only people wouldn't shout, Nick thought. He closed his eyes.

'Listen to me!' She was shaking him. 'Don't just sit there like a melting jellyfish. You've got money – a couple of weeks' pay, and that cheque from your uncle – why don't you *do* something?'

'Like, *live*?' enquired Nick bitterly. 'Shovel in baked beans every four hours? Have a shit? Pay the rent? Great. What a turn-on.'

'No, *not* like that. Do something different. Go abroad or something.'

'Huh.'

'It doesn't have to cost a packet. You could hitch.'

Nick's mind, against his will, darted back to the cab of the Scania, and he felt a flicker of interest. He dismissed it. 'Then what?' he said gloomily.

110

'I don't *know*!' Sasha shouted. 'Does it matter? It's better than sitting here playing at corpses! I can't go on like this, Nick,' she added more soberly. 'All this boredom and fed-upness – I know it's not your fault, but it makes you an awful person to be involved with.'

'You don't have to be,' said Nick ungraciously.

'I know that, too,' said Sasha, and he remembered her dancing with Roger at the party. Perhaps she really was look-ing for someone else. Perhaps this was an ultimatum. Get your act together, Cartwright – or else. 'I don't *want* to be beastly to you,' she went on, 'but – '

More to shut her up than anything, Nick pulled her on to the bed. Kissing her, he found himself thinking of plastic flowers in a holder on the dash. Aberdeen. Paris, perhaps. Istanbul. Where *was* Istanbul?

Maurice appeared at the open door, fork in hand. 'You want a sausage?' he enquired, surveying them. 'Pardon if I'm inter-rupting.'

'Yeah, I want a sausage,' said Nick recklessly. Since his privacy had been irrevocably disrupted, he might as well eat.

'Risen from the dead,' said Maurice, and nodded at Sasha with some respect. 'Looks as if you worked the oracle.'

'You won't have enough sausages for three,' said Sasha, standing up and dusting her skirt with her hand. 'I'll go down to the take-away and get some Jamaica patties or something. And some chips.'

Oh, chips, thought Nick, suddenly ravenous. He hauled his jeans on and pushed his arms into his new sweater with the sheep running round the bottom. 'Hang on,' he said. 'I'll come, too.'

Chapter 12

The ship's wake spread out in a long, crumpled path across the grey sea and Nick stared at it in panic. Now I've bloody done it, he thought. Goodbye, England. Oh Christ.

It had seemed easy enough, talking about it to Sasha in the cosy safeness of Ron's café. Easy, and not quite real. The sense of remoteness which had overcome him at the party had lasted all the time while he got himself a boat ticket, found out about getting a passport, sat in a photo cubicle in Woolworth's while the light flashed four times. The strip of four faces one above the other looked blank under the untidy hair, as anonymous as a refugee, or as one prisoner among many. And somewhere, un-admitted below the immobility of his mind, there was a bub-bling, childish excitement. In a romantic imagining, he sipped something long and cool while a fan circled slowly under the ceiling and a blue sea shimmered outside.

Rain began to blow in the wind, and Nick shouldered the rucksack he had borrowed from Paul Brent and made his way past the lifeboats to one of the doors which led to the inside of the ship. He pushed it open, stepping over a high sill. The ship was rather like a travelling pub, he thought. Brass edges to the carpeted stairs, plastic seats, video games. In the saloon, the barman was pushing up the grilles above the counter. Nick bought himself a lager and sat down with it.

After a while, Nick went up on deck again to see if there was any sign of France. To his surprise, it was quite close, near enough to see a line of houses along the sea front, and yet it took some time before they were approaching the harbour. The fine rain was salty-tasting, and the sea merged with the sky in greyness. This was not what Nick had expected. France was supposed to be sunshades over café tables, and waiters in white aprons playing piano-accordions.

The road which led away from the docks was wide and somehow shapeless. It ran through an open landscape of concrete, punctuated by occasional pale, square buildings, but casually, as if it didn't lead anywhere. Its surface had at one time been cobbled, and the square stones showed through their coating of tarmac, glistening with rain. The traffic driving on the right-hand side of the road made everything seem back to front, and there was a curious absence of solidness. Compared with the weighty façades of Dover, this place seemed temporary and inconsequential.

Beyond a general intention to head south and find some sunshine, Nick had no plans. He had sat gazing at the maps of France in the atlas David Bowman had given him, but the names remained meaningless. A squat concrete signpost in front of him announced, '*Centre Ville. Toutes Directions*'. Nick frowned at it, trying to decide what it meant. He had an idea that '*ville*' was French for 'town'. In that case, you probably had to go through the town, no matter which way you wanted to go after that. He set off again, pleased with himself for this deduction. The rain-misted air smelt very French, he thought. Cigars and coffee and – he suspected – shit. But somehow it wasn't unpleasant.

A bike with GB plates on it went past, with driver and pillion passenger in orange waterproof suits, and Nick felt a stab of envy. He wondered again if he had been stupid to give in to Sasha's insistence on some kind of action. With the money he had scraped up for this trip, he could have bought some kind of old bike. He'd even been to look at one or two, but they'd been well knackered. All the same, it was galling to be legging it along the pavement like some under-privileged wally.

A Renault 30 pulled up beside him, splashing water over his feet from the puddle in the gutter. Its window purred down and the driver spoke to him in rapid French. Nick stared at him, trying to make out what he was saying. The woman in the passenger seat frowned at the small boy in the back, who had chipped in with what Nick knew to be a cheeky comment.

'English?' asked the driver.

'Yes,' said Nick.

'You go where? Rouen? Paris?'

'Don't mind,' said Nick with a big French shrug. 'So long as it's on the way to the south.'

'We go to Abbeville,' said the man.

'That'll do,' said Nick. He opened the rear door and got in beside the small boy, who stared at him curiously, chewing. Anything was better than trailing about in the rain, Nick thought. And Renault 30s were pretty good cars. He leaned forward slightly and said, '*Merci*.'

'*Je vous en prie*,' said the man politely.

It must be weird to have a father with good manners, Nick thought as he settled back in the comfortable car. Unbidden, his mind went back to the previous day. There had been another row about the state of the walls. Maurice had dug his heels in about the Spring Mist, and the deadlock had not been resolved by the time Nick had left, so the graffiti had remained, unobliterated. Maurice had not said good-bye to him this morning. 'Hope you'll learn a bit of sense,' he had said, with his pale blue eyes bulging resentfully in his red face. 'Bloody stupid spending your own money on seeing the world, though. You ought to join the Army. They'd take you there free. *And* make a man of you.'

'Make a bloody moron, more like,' Nick had retorted.

'Oh, bugger off,' his father had snarled. Then, as Nick picked up his pack, 'And send us a postcard.'

'You'll be lucky,' Nick had said. And that had been that.

Now, in the back of the Renault, he felt irritable. Why think about Maurice? That's what he had come to get away from. He stared out across France. It was disappointing. Green and muddy and wet, with occasional small houses at the road's edge. It wasn't much different from the bleaker parts of Kent. And yet, the square, blue-edged signs with street-names on them were definitely foreign, and he saw an old woman in a doorway, wearing a black dress, with a scarf over her head, and she was foreign, too, like the Italian grannies he saw sometimes down the Elephant market. But it wasn't the kind of stuff you could write a postcard about.

The man stopped the car in Abbeville and said, 'This is the best place for you to get down. We go to our house now. From here, you can go to Rouen, or to Paris.'

'South?' queried Nick, getting out.

They all nodded patiently. 'South, *oui*, yes.'

Nick shut the door, 'Well, thanks a lot,' he said.

Waving, they drove off.

The rain had stopped but the sky was still grey. A clock on a church tower said twenty to five. Nick was very hungry. He found a supermarket which looked very much like a Tesco's, and went in, ranging along the shelves with a wire basket. The bread smelt good – long loaves standing end up in a bin, and a lot of other kinds on the shelves – but he settled for rolls as being easier to deal with. Butter would be too messy, but he bought cheese from an immense variety which, confusingly, didn't seem to include Cheddar, and a small hard sausage. He added some tomatoes and a couple of big peaches. All the stuff looked very classy, he thought. Then he came across a counter of amazing goodies, made-up open sandwiches better than any he'd seen, and mouth-watering cakes and pastries.

'I'll have one of those, please,' he said to the assistant, pointing to something covered with cherries and cream and red stuff.

'*Celle-ci?*' The woman pointed with white plastic tongs.

'Yes, please.' He didn't like the pitying look she gave him as she put the cherry thing into a bag and wrote the price on it. Just because he didn't speak Frog.

At the check-out he peeled off one of the notes Sasha's father had supplied through the Bank, together with travellers' cheques. 'Avez-vous a carrier?' he asked the girl. 'Carrier bag?' He described one with his hands.

'*Sac*,' said the girl reprovingly, pointing to a stack of rough-ish grey paper carriers. She snatched one up and piled his goods into it.

'Ta,' said Nick, and smiled at her. She tossed her head and pouted, but he glanced back as he made his way out, and saw her looking at him speculatively. She caught his eye and gave him a prim smile. Nick's spirits rose. France was all right, he decided.

He found a bench under a tree and ate his late lunch with enjoyment. Then he dug his map out of the rucksack, to see where he was. David's atlasses had been too bulky to bring, but Paul had lent him a rather dog-eared map. Peering at it, he decided that the Paris road looked a bit thin and insignificant. Perhaps he'd better stay on the N 28. The river which ran through the town was labelled, 'Somme'. So this was a first-world-war place, Nick realised. Barbed-wire territory. Good thing Maurice wasn't here. He'd be very boring about it. Nick got up, stuffed the map back into his rucksack, and started walking.

The town came to an end quite quickly, giving way to an open road with a line of trees growing along it. Nick turned to face the uncoming traffic, and stuck his thumb out.

An hour later, he was still there. He had taken off his rucksack and dumped it at his feet, and his arm ached mildly from holding it up. Car after car passed him, lorry after lorry. He tried the appealing smile, he tried an inward jerk of the thumb to draw attention to his presence, he tried bowing with his hand on his heart. Nothing worked. He cursed them all roundly, hating the feeling of being dependent on other people. For the first time, he dwelt fully on the loss of the Kawasaki and could not shrug it off. He had saved for months to get it, trading in his Honda Superdream as part of the bargain. And it had been brilliant. He had always wanted a 650, and the Kwacker was the one thing in his life which had been a complete, hundred-per-cent success. And now he was standing in the gutter like a prat, begging someone to take pity on him. To hell with the lot of them, he thought. He'd walk back into Abbeville and find the Youth Hostel.

He bent down for his pack, and at the same instant a green 2CV came to a halt beside him. 'Le Mans,' said the driver laconically, cigarette in mouth.

'Cheers,' said Nick, getting in. These were under-powered little turds of cars, but he wasn't fussing. 'That's really great,' he said. 'I thought I was stuck here for the night.'

'*Anglais?*'

'English, yeah.'

The driver made a face. '*Les anglais sont tous fous. Le foot-*

116

ball.' He shook his fingers as if they had been burned. '*Imbéciles.*'

'Oh, football hooligans, yeah, terrible,' agreed Nick. 'Load of idiots. Stupid.'

'*Stupides, oui,*' They seemed to have a lot of terms of abuse in common.

Nick tried to recall some of the words they had tried to teach him in those French lessons at school. *Je suis, tu es, il est. Je suis Nick,*' he said experimentally, tapping himself on the chest.

'*Vous vous appelez Nick?*' enquired the driver. '*Nicholas?*'

'No. Er – *non*. Dominic, Nick.'

The man seemed happy with that. '*Moi, je m'appelle Pascal,*' he said.

It was hard work, trying to find something to talk about. After a while Nick gave up. Apart from a brief foray into motor racing ('Le Mans, brrm-brrm, *oui*') he and the driver sat in silence as the car lurched its way through Rouen and out again into the open country.

It was evening by the time they approached the town of Le Mans, and the shadows of the trees lay in long bars across the road. Nick had not somehow expected France to be so big. The European atlas had managed to suggest that it was no larger than the British Isles, and yet they had been travelling for hours and nothing seemed to have changed.

Pascal pulled in to the forecourt of a *café routier* and parked the Citroen with the few other cars which stood among the lorries. '*Manger,*' he explained with knife-and-fork gestures. Nick was hungry, but the question of where to spend the night was large in his mind. '*Manger,*' he agreed, 'then find Youth Hostel. *Auberge de la Jeunesse.*' Sasha had rehearsed him carefully in this translation. 'Sleep.' He momentarily laid his cheek on his hand, shutting his eyes.

Pascal waved the problem away contemptuously. '*Vous pouvez dormir ici. C'est bon marché. Café,* sleep, yes?'

'Oh. Right,' said Nick.

Pascal led the way in, and Nick saw that a number of lorry drivers had pushed the tables together to form a single very large one, and were discussing the menu noisily. The man who ran the place was filling their glasses with wine. Nick felt a slight panic. Wine? This must be a classy sort of caff. Not like an ordinary British tranny.

A woman in a white apron said, '*Bonsoir, messieurs*,' as Nick and Pascal sat down. She tore a length of wide paper from a roll and flung it over their table as a cloth, then put a basket of bread on it, salt, pepper, glasses and knives. In response to an order from Pascal, a bottle of wine followed.

'Cheers,' said Nick as Pascal filled his glass. Well, he thought, if he used all his money up, he'd just have to go home earlier, that's all.

'*Santé*,' responded Pascal.

The lorry drivers were organising a starter course, handing plates of assorted cold meats across the combined tables to each other, some of them putting up a finger to claim soup or some kind of smoked fish. They argued volubly about the wine, holding a glass up to squint at it critically and debating its quality with fingers pinched together to emphasise a point. Nick was astonished. Nobody in Ron's would dream of behaving with this kind of connoisseurship. Anyone who tried it would be sent up something rotten. But these truckers seemed to take it all perfectly seriously.

The menu was baffling. Faced with Pascal's enquiry as to what he wanted, Nick spread his hands helplessly. 'I don't know,' he said. 'I'll have whatever you're having.'

Pascal tried hard to explain what each dish consisted of, but Nick was no wiser. He shrugged and said '*Oui*,' to all suggestions until Pascal ordered for both of them. The meal turned out to consist of smoked trout soup followed by steak, chips and salad, then a little cream-thing in a pot, then cheese. They drank the bottle of wine and had a brandy each with their coffee and Nick closed his eyes in anticipated horror as the bill came. Last time he had taken Sasha out to a place in Soho it had cost him an arm and a leg.

To his astonishment, it was not much more than a good blow-out at Ron's would have cost him. He checked the bill again to make sure, translating the figures mentally into pounds while Pascal watched him with some concern. '*Trop cher?*' he asked, eyebrows raised as he rubbed fingers and thumb together in the age-old sign for money.

'No, it's great,' said Nick. '*Bon.*' He peeled off the necessary notes. The lorry drivers had lapsed into contented conversation over their coffee. Talk about do themselves well, he thought. He and Pascal were the only people left in the café apart from the drivers, one of whom waved an invitation to join them. Pascal got up readily, and Nick followed him and was introduced.

'Ah. Ingleesh!' There was laughter and more shaking of burnt fingers. Everyone in France seemed to think the Brits were mad, Nick thought indignantly. He'd better buy a bottle of wine. That would cheer them up.

It was surprisingly easy to communicate this idea. A bottle arrived at once, and glasses were refilled. One of the drivers spoke quite good English.

'You like France?' he enquired.

'Yeah. 'S great.'

'You are what? Student?'

'No. Mechanic.'

'Ah.' They nodded, considering this respectable. Nick had decided to keep quiet about being unemployed. Good advice was so boring.

'England no good,' said the driver firmly. He screwed a finger to and fro at the side of his head. 'English all crazy. Peoples don't work. Not serious.'

'Can't be serious, mate,' said Nick. 'Life's too much of a bloody mess.' They didn't understand. 'Things very bad,' he simplified. 'So do what? Laugh.'

The driver made a face. 'Is understandable, perhaps,' he said. 'But if things are bad, then peoples must work to change it. To laugh nice, but is no use.'

This was translated for the others, who nodded agreement. Nick saw that he wasn't going to escape without good advice, after all. Everyone seemed to have something to say on the subject of Britain's unsatisfactory state. Nick caught words which sounded like the French for 'education' and 'politics' but he

119

had no hope of following the discussion. It was all very surprising. He had thought of the French as being merely one breed of the generalised 'foreigners' who couldn't speak English and were a bit of a joke – but it was different here. London had shifted from being the centre of all things to a much more minor status. It seemed now to be a far-off capital of an island where things were in a state of permanent cock-up. Still – 'You've got to laugh,' he repeated obstinately.

They glanced at him without understanding, and continued their debate. After a while, Pascal glanced at his watch and got up. 'I go,' he announced, and held out his hand to Nick, who shook it, half getting up as well. He had not understood where Pascal was making for, and was uncertain as to whether he was expected to accompany him.

The English-speaking driver answered his unspoken question. 'He goes to his home. Small roads – forty, fifty kilometres. No good for you.'

'Stay here tonight?' Nick queried.

The driver nodded and the woman in a white apron emerged from behind the counter and said, 'Stay 'ere, yes. *Ça va bien, m'sieur.*'

After shaking hands all round, Pascal went out. Nick felt more alone without him, although he had not been able to understand much of what he said. After listening to the incomprehensible conversation for a bit longer, he got up and went over to the woman behind the counter, paid for his bottle of wine and understood with gratitude that she was offering to show him his room. He picked up his rucksack to follow her, thus provoking a round of hand-shaking from the drivers, all of whom seemed to find it necessary to wish him, '*Bonsoir.*'

The room was small and basic, the toilet along the corridor turning out to be a white ceramic hole in the ground with two ferociously criss-crossed foot-shaped stands on either side of it. Looking at the size of them, Nick reflected that French plumbers must think people had bloody great feet. 'Thank you,' he said to the woman who was still smiling helpfully at his elbow. He shook hands with her as well, just to show willing, and she giggled and said, '*Bonne nuit!*' Perhaps you only shook hands in public places, Nick thought. It was all very perplexing.

The woman went downstairs and, after using the china hole,

Nick went back into his room. He washed at the tiny basin in the corner, then peeled his clothes off and got into bed. He heard the drivers coming upstairs, still talking and laughing, their feet loud on the bare wooden treads. Doors banged and water ran and then, though he was hardly aware of it, there was silence.

Chapter 13

Nick had intended to make an early start, but when he went downstairs the next morning, the café was almost empty. A couple of drivers nodded and said, '*Bonjour*,' but he did not recognise them from the previous night, and suspected that they had called in for a mid-morning break rather than breakfast. After milky coffee served in a bowl, and a couple of crusty rolls with apricot jam, he paid his bill and shook hands again with the woman in the white apron. 'Good-bye,' he said. '*Au revoir*.'

'*Au 'voir, m'sieur. Bon voyage.*'

Nick went out and set off along the road, but was soon overtaken by a lorry which pulled up ahead of him and waited until he caught it up.

'*Vous montez?*' offered the driver's mate, opening the door of the cab. Nick recognised the men who had spoken to him in the café, and climbed in gratefully. 'Thanks,' he said. 'Where are you going?'

'Clermont,' said the driver, starting off again.

'Where's that? South?'

'*Sud? Oui.* You go where?'

'Monte Carlo,' said Nick at random.

'Ah.' The driver made no further comment as he accelerated up to a noisy but unambitious 80 kph. Nick arranged his feet as comfortably as he could in the space left by his pack. This was not a very big lorry, and the engine vibrated in its tunnel between the seats. There was a small figurine mounted in front of the windscreen, a man with a child on his shoulders. 'What's that?' Nick asked after a while.

'*St Christophe.*' The man sounded reproving. '*Vous n'êtes pas catholique?*'

'Catholic? No.' Barbie had been brought up as a Catholic, but had long lapsed from the faith, implanting in Nick no more than a faint embarrassment where religion was concerned.

'*Anglais,*' the driver's mate pointed out, as if being English explained all spiritual failures.

The driver nodded, and set about an explanation of St Christopher. 'He is the saint of *voyageurs,*' he said.

'Travellers,' Nick guessed.

'*Oui, c'est ça.* The child become more and more heavy, because is the Christ-child, heavy like a man, you know? To find if Christophe can – er – continue.'

'Like a sort of test?' Nick suggested. 'To see if he'd go on carrying him?'

'*Exactement.*' The driver seemed pleased with the word. 'To carry him. To travel is hard sometimes, you see. St Christophe give courage.'

'Great,' said Nick, losing interest. He couldn't imagine that travelling was hard, not in a modern truck. A bit noisy and bumpy, perhaps, but easy enough. He fished out his tin of tobacco and rolled a cigarette, and offered it to the driver who accepted it. Then he rolled one for the driver's mate and one for himself.

The day was sunny, and the cab grew steadily hotter. By the time they stopped for lunch at a café next to a filling-station, Nick was glad to get out and stretch, pressing his hands into his back to ease the ache which was developing. He had no idea what this place was called. It didn't seem to matter very much.

Lunch was a leisured affair, with thick soup, omelettes and chips and salad, followed by cheese and accompanied by wine and, to Nick's surprise, the drivers waved aside his efforts to pay his share. There was a small shop at the front of the café, so he bought some chocolate and a kilo of little red apples, and

122

three cans of coke. It wasn't much, but it showed willing, he hoped.

The drivers, he learned, were called Michel and Gérard. As they pulled away from the café Nick felt full of good cheer. This was the life. Bright, sunny day – and he was on his way to Monte Carlo. He rolled another round of cigarettes. Michel and Gerard made faces over them, but they didn't refuse.

'What time we arrive?' he enquired, having lapsed easily into a simplified form of English.

'*À Clermont? Envers six heures et demi,*' said Michel, who was now sitting on Nick's right, having handed the driving over to Gérard. 'Six hours and half.' He tapped his watch.

'Half-past six?'

'*C'est ça. Va bien?*'

'*Va bien.*' Nick repeated, not sure what it meant. Go well? It seemed to be a sort of French okay. He fished in his pack for the map and spread it out. Michel dabbed a finger on the small yellow patch signifying a town and said, 'Clermont.'

'Yeah,' said Nick, slightly disappointed. It didn't seem to be near anywhere. There was a big place called Lyon about six inches to the right, with motorways going through it like wires through a washing machine's brain-box, but it looked as if he'd be better to stay on the N 102 if he was making for Monte Carlo.

'*Autoroute,*' said Gerard, detaching a hand from the wheel to point at the red and yellow lines of the motorway on the map. '*Très cher.*' He rubbed fingers and thumb together. '*Péage.*'

'Motorways are free in England,' said Nick smugly as he folded up the map.

Michel grinned. 'So we all go live in England for free auto-routes? I don't think.'

Nick gave up. He didn't want to provoke another lecture on the inadequacies of Great Britain. In any case, it was getting steadily hotter, and the noise of the lorry's engine made conversation an effort. He handed out apples, and when they were eaten and the tins of coke had been drunk, there was nothing to do but stare out at the white road. Time passed. Gérard made occasional disparaging remarks about the cretinous nature of

car drivers. Small towns came and went, sometimes with tanta-
lising glimpses of awnings and shops, and tables under trees on
the pavement. Nick was almost inclined to ask Gérard to stop
and let him out. Despite another round of apples, he was very
thirsty, and the idea of sitting in the shade with a glass of beer
was immensely appealing — and yet he was caught up in the
drivers' tacit acceptance of the fact that you did not stop except
for recognised meal-breaks. The desination had to be reached.
The plastic of the seats was hot to touch, the engine-housing
even hotter, but Michel and Gérard seemed unmoved. The
chocolate had been a mistake. It was almost liquid in its
packets.

The afternoon wore on slowly. The landscape had changed.
Everyone here seemed to grow sweet corn, Nick thought as he
stared out, and vines, in straight rows end-on to the road so
that they flashed by in stripes. The houses had shutters, and
pale, pinky-red roofs.

'In England, always the rain,' said Michel, breaking an
hour-long silence.

'Not always,' Nick objected. 'But very hot here. In England
not so hot.'

Michel shrugged. 'Not very hot now. In summer, yes, but is
okay now.'

If this cab was any hotter, Nick thought, it would be hell. He
glanced at the figure of St Christopher with more understanding, and dug the last of the apples out of their greyish
paper container.

The sun gradually dropped lower in the sky, flashing between the dark bars of the trees with rapid, dazzling monotony.
Nick had long ago given up shifting his position in search of
comfort. He sat in unresisting, aching inertia, with one foot
propped on top of his rucksack. The drivers had put the chocolate on the flat ledge which ran along behind the seats, so that it
would set into something like its original shape when it cooled.
Then he saw a road-side notice on the outskirts of a town which
said, Clermont-Ferrand.

'We made it,' he said over-colloquially.

'We arrive,' Michel remarked. He spoke to Gérard, who

nodded agreement, then explained, with some difficulty, that they were going to a factory on the other side of the town, and would leave Nick here so that he would still be on the main road.

'Yeah, great,' Nick agreed. '*Va bien.*'

Gérard brought the lorry to a halt outside a small café, and looked at his watch. After a few words to Michel he hit the Kill button and, as the engine shuddered to a stop, got out and pushed open the café door.

'We are a little bit early,' Michel explained.

'Time for a drink, then,' said Nick appreciatively.

'From here, you go to Le Puy,' said Michel. 'You speak with people in the café, someone take you.'

'Thanks,' said Nick, and hauled his pack out of the cab.

When they got into the café, Gérard was sitting at a table already supplied with three tall glasses of something cloudy and pale yellow, with ice in it. 'Cheers,' said Nick, taking a swig. He found that it was quite a strong Pernod.

They had another round of Pernod, which Nick bought, then Gérard stretched, running his fingers through his thin hair, and said, '*Alors. Faut partir.*' They stood up and first he then Michel shook Nick's hand. '*Bonne chance,*' said Michel. 'Good travel!'

'Thanks,' said Nick. '*Merci.* You've been great. And thanks for lunch and everything.' He mimed eating and said again, '*Merci.*'

They made dismissive gestures and went out. Good blokes, Nick thought. He heard the lorry start up and pull away. He tipped some more water from the yellow jug into his glass and swilled the ice cubes slowly. The Pernod had given him a definite buzz and he felt slightly and pleasurably dizzy. He rubbed the palm of his hand, cold from holding the glass, over his sweaty face.

He stayed in the café for some time, and drank all the water in the jug. It was marvellous to feel cool. After a while, he got up and went across to the door marked WC. He opened it and found a woman standing inside, applying lipstick before a fly-spotted mirror.

Nick recoiled. 'Sorry,' he said.

Unruffled, the woman said, '*Je vous en prie*,' and indicated the cubicle. Nick dithered uncertainly until she dropped her lipstick back into her handbag and went out, and even then he felt oddly insecure as he approached the china foot-stands visible through the cubicle door. Hoards of shrieking females might come bursting in at any moment. He was glad to get back to the café with no further embarrassment. The woman he had encountered took no notice of him, and continued to remonstrate mildly with a couple of toddlers for making a mess with their ice cream. Nick made a mental note not to be taken by surprise next time, nodded to the man behind the counter and said, '*Au revoir, monsieur*,' and went out. He was beginning to get the hang of this French thing.

After about ten minutes a man emerged from the café and went to his car, but he shook his head impatiently at Nick's tentative request for a lift. Humiliated, Nick walked off down the road angrily. Michel's advice didn't work, he thought. Asking people was too much like begging. He wouldn't try that again.

He kept on along the road for some time, then put his rucksack down under a tree. The sun was still warm, but the shadows were lengthening.

It was a very long wait. At last a battered Renault 4 van drew up and the driver, a very old man, opened the door for him. As the dilapidated vehicle set off, Nick enquired, 'Where are you going?'

'*Quoi?*' The old man turned rheumy eyes towards him.

Nick tried again. 'You go where?'

The old man launched into a torrent of spluttering explanation in incomprehensible French. He had very few teeth. Nick smiled at him and said, 'Okay, Grand-dad,' and gave up hope of conversation. At least he knew he was on the right road. But it was going to take some time to get to Le Puy at this rate. The old chap drove with all the verve of a woodlouse.

The sun was level with the horizon, scarlet and dazzling. The trees flicked slowly past, trunk after trunk after trunk. Nick watched them, half-hypnotised, and found himself thinking about Sasha. He had wished in London that she could come with him, but since he had been in France she had seemed to belong to another, far-away life. He felt a little guilty about it, but he could not imagine her sharing an experience such as this. In any case, how could she be fitted in? It would just about be possible, he supposed, but only if he went in the back of the van. Idly, he glanced over his shoulder, and found himself face to face with half a dead pig. The white eyelashes were peacefully closed over its single eye. The old man grinned and drew a finger across his own throat.

'Oh, great,' said Nick.

After nearly an hour, the old man slowed down and turned right into a narrow track, then came to a halt. Pointing, he explained (Nick guessed) that he lived in some remote hamlet over the hill and that Nick had better get out if he wanted another lift.

Mentally cursing, Nick clambered out and lugged his pack after him. '*Merci,*' he said.

The old man beamed at the sound of a recognisable word. '*Vous êtes anglais?*' he enquired.

'*Anglais, oui,*' said Nick stoically. At least if the old git was going to complain, he wouldn't understand him.

'*Ah, j'aime bien les anglais,*' said the old man, still beaming sentimentally. 'Winston Churchill. *La resistance, la guerre, le Maquis* – '

Nick had no idea what he was on about. But this crumbling old wreck, of all the French Nick had met, seemed to think the Brits were great. 'Yeah, well, thanks, Grand-dad,' he said. '*Au revoir.* See you.'

'*Au revoir, au revoir!*' And he burst into enthusiastic but unsteady song. 'God Sevv Ah Gree-shoose Quinn . . . .'

The quavering version of the British national anthem faded as the little van rattled away along the straight track which led between the fields, apparently to nowhere but the horizon.

Nick stumped bad-temperedly back to the roadside. The daylight was fading fast. Why hadn't the stupid old prat *said* he wasn't going as far as Le Puy? But then, he had to admit, in all that torrent of dribbling French, Nick wouldn't have known if

127

he *had* said. He fished the map out and tried to guess where he was, but there was not enough light to read by. He stuffed it back into his rucksack. A lot of the cars already had their lights on. He wondered why they used yellow bulbs, then noticed as the light faded further that the yellow road markings showed up as white in the cars' lights of the same colour. He tried to find this interesting, and failed. Standing there with his arm out like a human signal, his confidence began to wane. What was he doing here, anyway? What was the point of carrying one's fed-upness about? He suddenly felt a strong pang of homesickness for Ron's, where the warm, greasy smell was familiar and English did not have to be simplified.

His mind wandered while he smiled in failing hope at each of the passing cars. There had never been much point in anything, really. At school, the only point had been to get out of the place, but after that, the freedom had been short-lived. School had been replaced by the tyranny of time-clocks, the tedium of a week's mind-numbing work for the sake of a wage packet at the end of it. You were assessed purely in terms of potential output, as if you were a kind of human battery. Man-hours, productivity, efficiency. The worst thing was, you got into the habit of measuring yourself in the same way. Were you being successful? Could you point to tangible results? If not, there was nothing to be said about you at all.

Even here, Nick thought bitterly, on what was supposed to be a hang-loose holiday, he was stuck on the old business of trying to succeed. He'd set himself a little task, hadn't he? For homework, Cartwright, you will get to Le Puy.

An hour later, he was still waiting, and it was dark. He had known for a long time that it was useless. People didn't invite strangers into their cars at night. Sheer obstinacy had kept him there – that, and a reluctance to face up to the fact that there was no clear alternative. He was too far from Clermont to contemplate walking back. But he couldn't stand here all night. He shouldered his rucksack and started walking. With any luck, he thought, he would come to a village where he could spend the night.

He walked for a long time. The heat of the day seeped up

from the road's surface and the wash of air behind the occasional passing car whipped a scatter of dust against the legs of his jeans. A slip of a moon appeared, lying on its back indolently among wreaths of cloud. Fat lot of good that was, Nick thought, glaring at it. He had never been in such unrelieved darkness. He walked on, as if in a dream.

Dimly, he made out the shape of a roof against the sky. Approaching more closely, he sensed rather than saw that he had reached a group of buildings, standing a little distance from the road, with some kind of courtyard in front of them. He began to make his way towards them. Then he was aware of a large, warm presence close in front of him, and stopped dead. The hair was rising on his scalp. 'Who is it?' he whispered.

Grasshoppers continued their scratchy, voiceless song, and the thing in front of Nick was silent. Cautiously, he put out his hand in the darkness and touched it. His fingers came in contact with a hard, dry surface, perceptibly warm. It was, he realised, a huge pot, nearly man-high.

The little moon sailed free of its clouds, and in the resulting less-than-blackness, Nick perceived that he was surrounded by a silent population of the great terracotta pots, still warm from the day's sun, or maybe even from the kiln. He moved among them carefully, feeling their glowing warmth in the chill of the night. He found smaller ones standing on a rack of shelves by the wall of the building. It was weird, he thought, and laughed aloud.

A dog began to bark frenziedly and Nick heard a chain rattle and tighten with a thud. A window slid up and the dog went on barking. A man's voice shouted something, but Nick did not feel that it was the dog he was shouting at. For God's sake, he thought, I'm not going to steal your blasted pots. A right idiot he would look, trying to hitch a lift while he was lugging a thing like that. Clouds covered the moon again and the courtyard sank back into almost total darkness. Nick heard the dog's chain slide a link or two as it stopped barking. He could imagine it lying down, but with its ears still pricked. Very quietly, he felt his way between the pots, back to the road.

He could not walk for very much longer. He was hungry, but

the likelihood of finding a place where he could eat was getting remote. He regretted the chocolate, left behind in the lorry's cab. And he was very tired. The fitful moonlight showed him that bushy things were growing beside him in the fields, but he could not guess what they were. Maize plants, probably, or sunflowers or vines, judging by what he had seen all day. *Vines*, he thought with renewed interest. Would they have grapes on them? In curiosity rather than hope, he picked his way across the scrubby grass verge and felt along the leafy growth. Sure enough, a heavy bunch of fruit came to his hand. He pulled off a single grape experimentally, and put it in his mouth. It was deliciously sweet. He tore off the bunch and dumped his pack on the ground, sitting down beside it to give his full attention to the business of eating.

He licked his fingers when he had finished, and resolved to buy one of those plastic bottles of water the next day, when he found a shop. *If* he found a shop. There was no point in going any further tonight. He might as well stay where he was. Sitting on the grass, he patted around him in a broadish circle to see if it grew a bit more abundantly anywhere else, and decided it didn't. This was it, then. Bed-time. He dug in his rucksack and found his sweater, which he put on, then hauled out the obligatory YHA sheet sleeping bag and spread it out on the ground to lie on, with his rolled-up spare pair of jeans as a pillow. Then he lay down.

Something was rustling in the grass near his ear. He turned on his other side. The ground was incredibly hard. He lay still, trying to go to sleep. He wondered if it would be better if he took his shoes off. There was a stone under his shoulder, and he wriggled experimentally, trying to find a smoother patch. Something flew into his face and he dashed it off irritably.

After a while, he turned on his back and stared up. The clouds had cleared and the sky was full of stars. He might be anywhere, he thought. Nobody knew where he was, nobody could get in contact with him. He himself didn't know what this place was.

As tiredness slackened his limbs, he realised with a sudden, weakening sense of relief that there was no need to know. It did not matter.

Until now, the idea that nothing mattered had always been a depressing one, but this time it was different. He was lying here, at the edge of some field in France, and the fact that he felt the weight of his own body on the ground beneath him, and could see the array of other worlds out there in the infinite darkness, was enough. Here, at last, there was no measuring or assessment. No success, no failure. It did not matter if he never got to Monte Carlo, or even to Le Puy. The fact of simple existence was enough. Present moments succeeded each other endlessly. It was complete.

Why, he wondered, were things not complete all the time? It seemed sad now that so much effort and bother went into struggling with things. He thought of Maurice with his hopeless, stupid anger, and wondered if he had ever, during those long-dead Army days, which he seemed to look back to as some golden age, lain in a field and looked at the stars. Had he known an experience like the one which was happening to Nick now? Had he sought ever since to recapture it? Nick resolved to ask him, when he got back. He remembered the naked glance which had passed between them in the candle light of the birthday cake, and felt a regret that the truth which lay behind the glance was something he had never understood. Something Maurice himself had no words to express.

Nick let his mind run ahead to the future which awaited him. Whatever it was, it would not be easy to hold on to this feeling that the present was enough. And yet, it was something which he would never entirely forget. It would be there, tucked away for reference, like the knowledge of how to ride a bike or how to swim. In fact, Nick thought drowsily, it was not unlike that moment when, for the first time, you pushed away from the wall and trusted your weight to the water. He turned on his side and began, in his imagination, to swim.

It was dawn when he woke. He was very cold. The vines were wet-frosted with dew and a heavy mist lay across the fields. He curled up more closely, crossing his arms to tuck his hands into his armpits, and shivered. He wished he had a blanket.

Sleep would not come again and it seemed now, in the memory of many painful adjustments to the stony ground, that he had not slept at all. Stiffly, he got to his feet. The sheet sleeping bag lay uselessly twisted on the ground, and he picked it up and shook it, then folded it roughly. He stood hugging it to his chest, trying to flatten it out a bit, and saw in the grey morning light that the place he had slept in had no feature which made it a recognisable place at all. It was truly anonymous. No trees grew near, and there was no cart track or fence or ditch to mark it out from the surrounding landscape. He would never recognise it again. Even the flattened grass where he had lain was recovering itself as he looked at it. He did not mind. But he could not stop shivering.

He crammed the sleeping bag into his rucksack together with his spare jeans and heaved the thing on to his shoulders. Then he set off along the road as fast as he could make himself walk, in a kind of rapid shamble.

In less than a mile, he came to a village.

Chapter 14

Later that day, in a town called St Etienne, Nick bought a bottle of Evian water and a couple of postcards. He borrowed a pen from the ones on sale and wrote Sasha's address on one of the cards. Then he put, 'Didn't mean to come here but it doesn't matter. Going to Monte Carlo I think. Very good grapes in fields.' He paused, then added, 'No accordions.' He hoped she would understand what he meant — that France wasn't just blue berets and striped umbrellas and waiters playing accordions. He couldn't explain it on a postcard. He hoped he hadn't made any spelling mistakes. Sasha was inclined to be superior about spelling. He hesitated over Maurice's card. In the allocated square, he couldn't touch on the questions he wanted to ask. And anyway, Maurice wouldn't be expecting to read anything that mattered. It was going to be quite tricky, trying to get any straight answers out of him, even when Nick got back. He wrote, 'Having a great time,' in large letters, to take up the space, then, through the habit of being annoying, added, 'Saw the Somme. No barbed wire – funny.' He signed his name on the bottom of both cards and added a row of crosses on Sasha's, returned the pen to its section of the counter and went in search of stamps and a post box.

Tasks completed, he set off again, walking out of the town on the white, dusty road. It had not been a bad day so far, he thought. The village he had come to at dawn had boasted a café which, miraculously, was open, and the proprietor had given him a glass of wine heated by putting it under the coffee machine's steam pipe. A bit of cackling and grunting had conveyed that Nick wanted bacon and egg, which had arrived cooked all together on a metal dish, with lots of fresh bread, and then there had been the ride in a dilapidated Renault 12, which had brought him to St Etienne.

To Nick's irritation, he saw that a girl in shorts was already standing at the road's edge, thumb extended. That put him a poor second, he thought. People were much more willing to give a girl a lift.

As he drew level, the girl said, 'Hi!' and grinned at him.

'You're English!' said Nick. It was marvellous to be able to speak to someone who understood him.

'New Zealand,' the girl corrected. She had brown curly hair and wore a yellow vest over her shorts, which were jeans with the legs hacked off. 'You a Britisher?'

'Yeah, from London.'

'I'm from Christchurch. Where you been?'

Nick told her, and she nodded and said, 'Oh, you just started. I came down from Amsterdam a couple of days ago but I went to see some people I met who've got a house near Limoges. Thought I might as well, while I was in Europe.'

'Where else have you been?' asked Nick.

She reeled off a list of countries. Greece, Turkey, Bulgaria – 'Istanbul's quite a place,' she commented at that point – Yugoslavia, Austria, Germany, Holland, Belgium . . . .

'So where are you heading for now?' asked Nick, interrupting the flow rather firmly. Where *was* Istanbul?

'Oh, little place, near Marseilles. I said I'd meet some friends there.' She made it sound like popping over to Fulham. 'What about you?'

'I thought I'd go to Monte Carlo,' said Nick. 'But I don't know.'

The girl made a face. 'Okay if you're rich,' she said. 'Or if you like watching glamorous people. Trouble is with that coast, you can't get near the water except in the grotty bits where it's stony. The rest of it's all pay-beaches, fenced off for the hotels.'

'Looks like I'm not going *there*, then' said Nick, without much regret. 'What's Marseilles like?'

'It's okay,' said the girl. 'People say it's a rough town, but I like it. And there's a good Youth Hostel there. Are you hostelling?'

'I joined the YHA,' Nick admitted, remembering Sasha's insistence that he should do so, 'but I haven't made it to a hostel yet. I slept in a field last night.'

She did not seem surprised. 'Can't always get to a town, can you. Don't you carry a tent?'

'I will next time,' said Nick. He found that he took it as a definite assumption that he was going to do a lot more of this travelling.

'Well worth it,' said the girl. 'They don't weigh a lot. Do you want to come with me, far as Marseilles? I'd quite like someone to hitch with. The blokes down here can get a bit funny.'

'Don't they get funny everywhere?' asked Nick. This girl didn't have Sasha's striking looks, but her freckled face was pretty in a straightforward way, and her sunburned legs were long and slim.

'Not as much as they do in the south,' said the girl. 'I reckon it's the sun makes them randy. They're okay in the Iron Curtain countries, though. Ever so polite. Desperate to get their hands on hard currency, but they keep them off everything else.'

Nick was tempted to try some merry quip about Siberia, but

decided against it. She might have been there, too. 'What's your name?' he asked.

'Jenny. Yours?'

'Nick.'

Jenny had kept a hopeful thumb extended during this conversation, and a large Mercedes truck came to a halt a few yards down the road. They picked up their packs and ran towards it.

After that, things seemed to fall into place of their own accord. Near the harbour in Marseilles, Jenny met some people she knew. ('Hi! Where have you been since Piraeus?') They offered a lift to Jenny's 'little place' in an old van, and it seemed assumed that Nick would go along, too.

They left the van on a rough concrete area beside a beach café and walked for a long way across the sand dunes until they came to a makeshift camp by the sea. It was not exactly Butlins, Nick thought with relief as he surveyed the sun-bleached tents and the less orthodox structures of polythene and bits of wood. For two pounds, he bought a brown-and-white patterned blanket from an American girl who was going home, and that night, lying on an unravelling straw sand-mat which Jenny had salvaged from a litter bin outside the beach café, he slept soundly.

The next morning, he was covered with mosquito bites. A young man carrying a yellow plastic water container surveyed him with some concern and said in careful English, 'There is place in our tent if you wish for shelter tonight.'

'Thanks,' said Nick.

From then on, the days were idyllic. The people in the camp were of all nations, but there was between them a tacit understanding of why they were there. Nick was not alone in his experience of boredom and crushing depression – or, he discovered, in the acceptance which had come to him during his night under the stars in France. It was implicit in the simplicity with which they lived. They swam, walked across the hot sand to the little shop-cum-café to buy bread and wine and fruit, swam again, then ate, and afterwards sought refuge from the

135

heat of the day in any shady place, dozing like cats until the late afternoon. But it was the end of September, and when the sun dropped behind the smooth, glistening sea, its warmth was suddenly gone, and the nightly bonfire on the beach became more of a necessity. The work of the day was a constant scrounging of driftwood and of rubbish from the café – anything which would burn.

Nick came to know a lot of people slightly, a few of them well. There was Jenny, to start with, and her friends Chrissie and Pam, and the German boys whose tent he shared, Dieter and Hansi. A cheerfully profane Australian called Bob became a particular friend, along with Carlo, who said very little but played his guitar almost endlessly. Nobody listened to him during the day, but nobody asked him to help collecting wood, either, and at night his music was there, along with the lapping of the small waves on the beach, as a kind of assurance that this place, for all its ephemeral nature, was their home.

But the summer was almost over. The days were short now, and people started to drift away like birds answering the imperious call of migration time. Bob went back to Australia to start the summer season there on the proceeds of his months of selling ice cream to tourists, and Dieter and Hansi began to pack up their few possessions to return to Germany for the beginning of the university year. And Nick's money finally ran out. It had lasted much longer than he had imagined it possibly could, but the day came when, with a few francs left for the return journey, it was his turn to say good-bye.

He exchanged addresses with the sunburned, bare-footed people who had, for a short time, been so close, and the laborious spelling of foreign towns and street names turned them into strangers again. Then he walked for the last time across the warm, sliding sand, pushed his beach mat back into the bin it had come from, and set out on the long track to the road. He was on his way back to what they called civilisation.

That night, in a town called Vienne, he ate the bread and cheese he had bought at the beginning of the day from the beach café, then rolled himself in his blanket and lay down on a bench under a tree in a quiet square. He slept soundly, and woke the next morning to find an impassive man sweeping up yellow poplar leaves with a twig broom. There were a lot of leaves on Nick himself. Babes in the bloody wood, he thought. He felt a painful sense of loss, though whether for childhood or for the summer, he could not say.

The journey back across France was tedious. The weather grew colder as he travelled north, and the landscape drabber. In gathering darkness, he stared out of a lorry window. This time, the First World War atmosphere was stronger. They passed a cemetery where the pattern of neat white headstones covered acres and acres of ground, like some enormous chequer-game where all the men were losers. Everything seemed to smell hauntingly of mud. Roses are blooming in Picardy, Nick thought, remembering the wistful tune from the television programme Maurice had been watching in that far-off time before the bike was stolen. Pink, scented, beautiful roses, in all that green-grey mud. It was enough to make you weep. He began to look forward to getting home.

Chapter 15

Nick dropped off the bus on which he had done the last stage of his journey as it paused at a zebra crossing, and started walking towards his flat. The estate looked incredibly dirty, he thought. Ugly, too. The buildings seemed lumpish and crude. He felt a fresh and urgent desire to own a bike again. Idling in France, it had been easy not to care. Here, there was a need to fight back.

As he approached his block, Nick did some calculation to confirm his vague feeling that it was a Saturday. And, probably, it was October by now. In the last weeks, it had not mattered what the date was, but now he would need to fit in again with other people's marking of the passage of time. Saturday. Mid-afternoon. Maurice would be watching the sport on television. Nick ran up the steps to the first walkway, and was lucky with the lift. A few minutes later, he was fitting his key into the front door.

'Dad!' he shouted. 'Hi! I'm home!'

There was no answer, and no sound of television from the living-room. Nick felt a surge of anger. Not again, he thought. Bloody charming home-coming this was, if the old sod was flat out after another booze-up. There were a lot of letters lying on the mat at Nick's feet, and he bent to pick them up. Maurice must have had a hell of a night if he couldn't even totter out to collect the mail, he thought. Among the letters was the post card he had sent from France, foreign now with its lurid blue sky. Talk about slow, only arriving today after all that time. Thank you, Post Office. When he'd written that card, he hadn't imagined he'd have to be in the room with Maurice when he read it. He wasn't going to like the crack about the Somme and the barbed wire.

Nick went into the living-room and put the letters down on the table. It was odd that there were such a lot. Everyone had suddenly gone writing mad. He grinned when he saw that the walls had been painted over with Spring Mist. He'd won, he thought. Even if the felt-tip graffiti *were* coming through. He'd have to be tactful about that. Mustn't rub the old boy's nose in it.

He dumped his pack on the floor and bent down to undo its buckles, then got out the bottle of whisky he had bought at the duty-free shop on the night boat. He ought not to have brought whisky for Maurice, he thought. It was only encouraging him. But there'd been nothing else he'd want. He didn't like cigars or chocolate, and Nick could hardly have brought him one of those poxy little dolls in national costume.

Holding the bottle, he pushed open his father's bedroom door. The room was empty, the bed, as usual, unmade. Nick frowned. He looked in the bathroom, glanced into his own room then went into the kitchen to see what time it was. Could

138

'The Plumbers' still be having a late lunch-time session? The clock on the cooker said a little past quarter to five. Maurice must have gone out for some shopping, then. Funny he didn't pick up the mail.

Nick put the bottle of whisky down on the draining board and went back into the living-room where he had left the letters. Most of them were rubbish. An advert for water softeners, an offer to 'Develop Your Films Free', the electricity bill. There was a letter postmarked Esher which was probably from Walter and Enid, and a couple addressed to himself. One, unstamped and delivered by hand, was in Sasha's writing. The other was white and official. Something about the bike, he thought hopefully. He tore it open.

The letter had an official heading with a lot of printed information which Nick didn't stop to read. 'Dear Mr Cartwright,' it said, 'I very much regret to inform you that on the evening of September 16th your father, Mr Maurice Cartwright, was involved in a traffic accident. He was taken to St Thomas's Hospital but unfortunately was found to be dead on arrival. I am sorry to have to bring you such sad news in this way, but our efforts to contact you were unsuccessful and I understand that you were out of the country.' There was quite a lot more. Something about contacting a social worker.

Nick sat down on the arm of the chair. For God's sake, he thought. Why now? He wasn't prepared. It was the wrong time. The flat's emptiness of Maurice suddenly seemed an ugly, positive thing, a sort of blackness. Nick felt very weak. The sense of interruption was outrageous. 'Thank you, *God*,' he said aloud. There were things he had wanted to say to Maurice. Things he needed to ask him. And now it was too late. His chest hurt. His heart seemed to be thumping painfully.

He got up and went into the kitchen, and stood there irresolutely. His joints seemed to have turned to water. The duty-free whisky still stood on the draining board, and Nick opened it and poured a little into a mug. The harsh taste made him feel fractionally stronger, though it did nothing to still the torrent of protest in his mind. Why *now*? Anger stood like a figurehead in front of a looming bulk of grief. He put the mug down and stood with his clenched fists resting on the edge of the sink. For a long time, it seemed impossible to move as his thoughts turned and twisted in an agonised effort to take in what had happened to him. He felt very cold. At last he remembered Sasha's letter, and went slowly back into the living-room to open it.

'Darling, darling Nick, (she had written in her graceful sprawl).

'You are going to read this when you come back from abroad, and I don't know if there will be some other, official letter or not. I was going to put, just ring me straight away, and I do want you to do that, because I love you very much, and I want to do anything I can to help. But in case you're standing reading this in an empty flat and wondering what's happened, I'll have to tell you, there's been an accident. Your father got knocked down by a car. They said it was quite late at night, but I don't know anything more than that about the details. I heard about it from Barbie. She rang up because the police went round to see her, and she didn't know when you were coming back from France, and she thought I might know, but of course I didn't. I just said in about a fortnight if you could make the money last. I've never had to write a letter like this before, and I do so wish it didn't have to be you. Please do ring me when you've read this. Never mind if it's during the day, ring me at the Abrahams'. I told them about it and they were really upset, so they won't mind if you call. With lots and lots of love. Sasha.'

Nick folded the letter up slowly. She hadn't actually brought herself to mention the word, 'death', he thought. Perhaps she hadn't been able to decide whether to tell him Maurice was dead by writing it down or by waiting until she saw him. Her anxiety came from the pages like a stale perfume, sharp and uncomfortable. He went to the telephone and dialled her number.

'Hello?' It was Mrs Bowman. He could have done without that, he thought.

'Is Sasha in?'

'Oh, Nick, dear, you're back.' She sounded flustered. 'I'll call

140

her, just a minute,' There was the hollow noise of a hand being placed over the receiver, and distant shouting. Then her voice was in his ear again. 'I'm glad you're back.' She was taut with embarrassment. 'Er – have you had a nice time?'

'Yes,' said Nick. The world was insane.

Sasha's voice said, 'Oh, Nick.' She sounded distraught, and Nick felt a kind of possessive anger. Maurice hadn't been *her* father. 'It's all right,' he said, trying to calm her.

'You're at the flat?'

'Yes.'

'You found my letter?'

'Yes. Thanks for writing. There was one from the Social Services or someone, saying he was dead.'

'Oh. I didn't know how to tell you.'

'No. It's all right,' Nick said again. Her voice, so close to his ear, roused in him a great desire to be near her. The emptiness of the flat was suddenly unbearable. 'I want to see you,' he said.

'Listen,' said Sasha, 'Mum says you must come and stay with us for a bit. I mean, we can be together and everything. We've talked about that, and she doesn't mind. It's all organised.'

'Couldn't you just come over here?'

'Yes, of course, if that's what you want.' She would do anything for him, he realised. She loved him. Devastatingly, he was shaken by a rush of tears.

'Nick, darling, I'll be there very soon. Just hang on. I love you.' The receiver purred in his ear.

Nick went and lay on his bed and wept. Sasha had disarmed him, reduced him to a little boy wanting to be hugged and comforted. And somebody had to weep for Maurice. Poor old bugger, Nick thought, recovering a little. The crowd at the Plumbers' Arms would get drunk one more time in his memory, and that would be that. Nobody else would care. Nick wondered where he was. In some fridge at the hospital, he supposed. Unless there'd been a funeral and he'd missed that as well.

After a few more minutes he sat up. He felt overwhelmingly tired. Then he saw a letter addressed to him propped against the alarm clock. Maurice must have put it there where he would see it, he thought. Thanks, Dad. He had to overcome fresh tears before he could see what it said, and then found that it was from his insurance company, offering him less than half what the Kawasaki had been worth. Bastards, he thought. They weren't getting away with that. He'd stick out for the proper value. But the thought of the effort involved made him feel weak. He went slowly into the bathroom, where he washed his face and hands. He looked at Maurice's Steradent tablets on the shelf and nearly cracked up again. There was going to be such a lot of things to throw away. Or would he have to leave the flat? It had been in Maurice's name. He didn't know what the Council would do about that. Everything seemed to have fallen to bits.

The doorbell rang. He walked across the hall and opened the door, and a girl with beetroot-coloured hair said, 'Darling,' and hugged him tightly.

'You've changed your hair,' said Nick, aggrieved. It seemed one more stupid, insignificant example of the betrayal which had been going on behind his back. He should never have gone away.

Sasha went on hugging him. Freeing an arm, Nick pushed the door shut and said, 'Would you like some coffee? Only I don't expect there's any milk.' It was awful how everything sounded pathetic. He hadn't meant it that way. 'I brought you something from France,' he said, trying again. The yellow headscarf he had bought in the little store beside the beach café was somewhere at the bottom of his rucksack.

'Thank you.' She smiled up at him tremulously. Her face looked paler under the outrageous hair. 'Oh, Nick, it's marvellous to see you. Even though it's so sad.'

'Don't keep on,' said Nick. He was trying desperately to get used to the situation. To regard it as normal.

'No. I'm sorry. Look, you can't stay here all on your own, not till things are sorted out. Mum's downstairs with the car. You can come back with us.'

It was surprisingly tactful of Mrs B not to come up, Nick thought. He wandered into his bedroom to see if there was a clean shirt to wear at the respectable Bowman household. The contents of his rucksack needed washing, to put it mildly, and he hadn't got much else.

'Mum thought she'd better not leave the car because of vandals,' said Sasha.

Nick gave a kind of laugh. One more illusion dispelled. He hauled a sweat-shirt out of a drawer and found a clean pair of socks. 'Perhaps I could put some stuff in your washing machine,' he said.

'Yes, of *course*.' She gazed at him in eager willingness. He could do anything.

Before he went, he opened the rest of the letters. The one from Enid said, 'Dear Maurice, Walter and I have to thank you for the party on Saturday, though frankly, we were a little shocked by some of the behaviour we saw, not least your own. We trust that Dominic will appreciate the silver brushes. An occasion like a twenty-first should be marked by something a bit special, we thought.' Nick smiled briefly. Those had gone to a chap he knew down Leather Lane. Made enough for the boat ticket, anyway. 'We found that the car's aerial had been snapped off when we left your flat,' Enid went on, 'and an obscene message had been written on it with a spray can. So Walter and I feel in future that any meetings of the family would be better held in Esher. With our love, Enid and Walter.'

Nick passed the letter to Sasha. 'Shan't have to bother with them any more,' he said. Enid's letter would have caused a fearful outbreak from Maurice. The silence as Sasha read it was uncanny.

A second single bed had been moved into Sasha's small room, making it quite difficult to get in through the door.

'Mum thought you'd be more comfortable,' Sasha said apologetically. 'I couldn't say anything. It's quite a change for her to be able to talk about that sort of thing. I think she found your party quite — stimulating. Or perhaps it was facing up to meeting Dad. But she's been different since.'

Nick surveyed the neat beds now twinned in identical candlewick covers, and wished the woman had minded her own business. He had liked tumbling into the same bed with Sasha, waking in the morning curled together under her rumpled blankets and faded Indian bedspread.

'It's rather sweet, really,' Sasha went on. 'She met this man – he's quite a bit older than her, with a little grand-daughter he brings to the ballet class. She said he seemed terribly out of it. You can imagine, can't you. Those ghastly mums fussing with their darlings' hair-nets and crossover cardigans. They're going to a concert tomorrow.'

'The mums?' Nick had not been attending.

'No, twit. Mother and this bloke. He's called Geoffrey.'

'Good for her,' said Nick. He went across to the window and looked down into the garden, where the grass was covered with leaves from the ornamental cherry trees. He thought of the yellow poplar leaves in the square in Vienne, where he had not known that Maurice was dead. The accident was on the sixteenth, the letter had said. 'What's the date?' he asked.

'October the fifth,' said Sasha. 'Why?'

'Nothing,' said Nick. Then, relenting, he admitted, 'I was trying to work out exactly when it happened. Where I was at the time.' But he knew.

'It was the second night after you'd gone,' said Sasha.

He nodded, unsurprised, although he had almost hoped that she was going to prove him wrong. That night under the stars, Maurice had been in his mind strongly, and as a young man like Nick himself, not as the drunken old wreck he had become. But there was no hope of talking about that. It sounded too easy. As if he'd made it up.

Sasha came and twined her arms round his neck. 'Tell me about France,' she said. 'What did you do? Did you find some good Youth Hostels?'

'I never used one,' Nick admitted. 'It didn't work out that way.' He gave her a sketchy account of the journey. It sounded ludicrously disorganised, and after a while Sasha laughed. 'In fact, you've spent the last three weeks being a bum,' she said. 'But it sounds great. It must have been fun.' Her smile faded as she remembered what he had come back to.

'Yes,' said Nick. 'I suppose it was.' He wished there was some way to explain what it had really been like.

144

'Your postcard was brilliant,' said Sasha. ' "No accordions." That absolutely said it all. Demolished the conventional idea of Abroad in one fell swoop.'

'Really? Oh, great,' said Nick. 'I didn't know if you'd understand.'

Sasha stared at him gravely from sepia-shadowed eyes. He had almost forgotten how marvellous she looked. 'I never *quite* understand,' she said. 'I think that's why I love you. I couldn't ever be really interested in someone like Gary, because he'd never do anything unexpected. Sometimes it gets to be a bit much – that's why I hassled you into going off on this trip, I suppose. Partly because I can't bear it when you get into one of your states of gloom, but partly for a sort of breathing space.' She turned away to the mirror and pushed her maroon-coloured hair back from her face with both hands, looking at herself. 'I went out with Roger once or twice,' she said.

'I thought you would,' said Nick. 'You were with him all the time at the party.' He hoped she wasn't going to tell him anything he didn't want to know.

She turned to face him. 'He helped me buy a bike,' she said. 'A Honda 125. Only my licence hasn't come through yet, so I can't actually ride it.' She gave a nervous laugh. 'Silly, really.'

Nick felt a surge of outrage. 'I *told* you I'd help you find a bike,' he said.

'I know you did.' Sasha was defensive, but not apologetic. 'But I've had time to think about it. You've always said you don't want anyone depending on you. Remember that time in Kew Gardens? That's one of the reasons I wanted you to go away for a bit, to see how I felt, being without you.'

'And being with Roger,' said Nick childishly.

'I only went to the pictures with him,' said Sasha. 'And a couple of times for a drink. I didn't go to bed with him or anything.' She stared at Nick with steady candour. 'You were quite right. I do have to be more independent. I can see that now. So it's no good you being jealous – and you don't have to be, anyway.'

Nick scowled and said, 'I'm not.' He hadn't gone to bed with anyone, either, all the time he had been in France, but somehow he was reluctant to say so. 'What about this bike, then?' he asked, retreating to safer ground. 'You haven't gone and got stitched up with a load of rubbish, have you?'

'I don't think so,' said Sasha. 'Dad came and looked at it as well, and he thought it was a good buy.'

'Is it here?' asked Nick.

'Yes, in the garage. Only, like I said, I'm waiting for my licence to come from that place in Swansea.'

'The DVLC.'

'Yes. I ought to have sent off for it earlier, but I wasn't expecting to find a bike so quickly.'

Nick knew she wanted him to go and look at it, but he felt utterly inert. He spoke the word aloud in his own mind, with a mild curiosity about what was happening to him. Inert. The opposite of alert, like it said on the card in Len's garage. He was a nert. Sasha was looking at him with a troubled expression. 'Are you all right?' she asked.

'Yeah. Think so.' He didn't want to talk about how he felt. There was a wobbly uncertainty somewhere which was best left alone. 'Is Gary back from Sweden?' he asked.

'Oh, yes, they came back last week,' said Sasha. 'They're getting married next Saturday. There's going to be a party afterwards. Liz said would I tell you.'

'Yeah,' said Nick again. Nothing had changed, he thought. He wondered again when the funeral would be. Weddings and funerals. Until now, they'd just been boring little notices in newspapers. Big black cars driving slowly or be-ribboned ones scattered with confetti.

'Gary seems to have got some scheme afoot,' Sasha went on. 'I don't know if he's just gone all ambitious now he's going to be a married man, but he's talking about leaving Len's place.'

'Got another job, has he?'

'Not exactly. He's thinking about going self-employed.'

Nick gave a short laugh. 'Off his head,' he said. 'You need money for that sort of thing. And a workshop and equipment.'

'It's something to do with Paul Brent's father,' said Sasha. 'Apparently he's got an old funeral parlour or something behind the house.' She laughed, embarrassed. 'Not a very nice

146

thing to be talking about just now.'

Nick shrugged. He felt a moment's envy, remembering the evening when Mr Brent had told him he should set up in business. So Gary had got in first. Well, good luck to him.

Joanna Bowman served pancakes stuffed with prawns for the evening meal, and seemed concerned about Nick's lack of appetite. 'I expect it's the shock,' she said, gazing at him with grey eyes which must have been like Sasha's once, he thought. Now, she looked like an anaemic spaniel. The food in front of him smelt quite pleasant, but it seemed impossible to eat. His stomach felt full of heavy nothingness. 'I think you two had better get an early night,' said Joanna firmly.

She certainly had changed, Nick thought. And she was right about the early night. He ached with tiredness. It seemed a long time since the night crossing from Dieppe, where his last lift in France had landed him, and he had not slept for more than three hours on the boat.

Later that night, he lay beside Sasha, filled with tension, and wondered why he was still awake. He listened to the tranquil regularity of her breathing, and felt more alone than he had ever done in his life. After a while he eased himself gently away from her, murmuring a reassurance as she stirred slightly. He crept carefully out of the bed and went across to the window, where he pulled the curtain back and looked out. The moon hung in the city-lit, brownish-orange sky. It was past its fullness now, creamy-pink like a bland, lopsided face. It seemed a different thing from the little moon in France. Nick tried to think about Maurice. Death was supposed to be important, he told himself. Remembrance services, sonorous words, summings-up of the worth of the departed. He ought at this moment to be thinking something memorable. But he could find nothing.

Guiltily, he stared at the moon and fretted over the emptiness he felt within him. The autumn garden lay motionless in the cool grey light. There were no answers out there. No answers anywhere. Strangely, the thought was comforting. If there were no answers, then there was no need to ask questions.

147

He knew again that each moment was complete. Anxiety was irrelevant. It did not matter.

He let the curtain drop. His feet were cold. He went over to the newly-imported second bed and pulled the cover back, then slipped between the sheets. As they lost their chill, he fell deeply asleep.

Chapter 16

The next morning was terrible. Sasha and her mother looked after Nick with a solicitude which made him feel like an invalid, and this was particularly annoying as a good night's sleep had restored him to something approaching normal. He rang up his mother at midday, mindful of Tim's instruction not to disturb them during off-duty hours, and had a brief conversation against a background of cheerful pub noise, which made him wish he was there instead of being marooned among the chintz armchairs of Mrs Bowman's sitting-room. Barbie said she and Tim would be over at four, to discuss arrangements.

Joanna looked anxious when Nick communicated this news. 'Will they want a meal?' she asked.

'Oh, no,' said Nick. 'They'll have to get back for evening opening.'

Joanna nodded dubiously and said, 'It must be a terrible tie.' She hovered for a moment, then added, 'Would you like a sherry?'

'Yes, please,' said Nick. 'Sweet.'

Outside the French windows, his clothes were decorously exposed on the line, socks pegged side by side in pairs, jeans neatly straightened. Nick caught himself feeling defensive about their dilapidated condition. In the anonymity of the launderette, it was nobody else's business, but here, he could not escape from knowing that Sasha's mother had carefully shaken out and hung up the faded tee shirts and unsavoury socks, and that pair of pants which was coming undone along the seams. And then he was annoyed with himself for letting it bother him. If he chose to spend his money on running a bike rather than buying snazzy underwear, that was his business. Or rather, it used to be.

Sasha sat curled in an armchair, reading the colour supplement from one of the Sunday papers. The rest of the paper lay on the polished table in the squares of sunlight which slanted in through the windows. A modern kind of small grandfather clock ticked slowly in the corner; otherwise the room was very quiet. Michaelmas daisies bloomed in tidy clumps in the garden. Nick turned away from the window and perched uneasily on the arm of the chair, with his hands pushed into his pockets.

'What's the matter, love?' asked Sasha, looking up.

Nick shook his head. Everything was the matter. The house oppressed him with its calm comfort and its faint smells of polish and gravy. 'Mum said the funeral's on Friday,' he said evasively. 'At the crematorium in Croydon.'

Sasha looked sympathetic and asked, 'What time?'

'Quarter to eleven,' said Nick. After a pause while he thought about the significance of this, he added, 'I suppose they get through four corpses an hour.'

'How awful,' said Sasha, distressed. Then she looked at him and added, 'I don't think Mum will like you sitting on the arm of the chair, darling. She always used to scold me about that. She says it weakens them or something.'

Nick tumbled untidily into the chair's seat as Joanna came in with the drinks on a tray. He couldn't stay in this place much longer.

'Charming house you have here, Mrs Bowman,' said Tim genially as he and Barbie came into the room. Anyone would think he was a bloody estate agent, Nick thought.

'Joanna,' corrected Sasha's mother.

'Yes, of course,' said Tim, still sounding hearty. 'Joanna.' He smiled kindly at Nick, who realised that the *bonhomie* was for his benefit. The verbal equivalent of a bunch of grapes for the invalid, who was suffering from the embarrassing disease of bereavement.

Barbie didn't say anything. Nick saw her glance round the room in shrewd appraisal, and grinned to himself. She looked outlandish in this tasteful setting, with her tumbling dark hair and her eyes boldly outlined with mascara. Perhaps as a tribute to Maurice, she wore a black roll-neck sweater with a diamante brooch pinned to the shoulder, but her pink mohair skirt was too short to pull over her knees as she perched on the edge of the sofa, her feet placed to one side so as to accommodate the high heels of her tight-laced boots. She met Nick's eyes as Joanna went out to the kitchen, and spread her hands helplessly. There was no need for words. The sadness lay in knowing that there was no chance now for any explanation or new understanding. It probably wouldn't have happened anyway, but there was no uncertainty about it now. Maurice was fixed for ever, in the past.

'You'll be able to keep the flat on if you want to, Nick,' Tim told him. 'I've made enquiries at the Council.' Despite his avuncular manner, Nick detected a trace of impatience in his voice, and remembered that he had been pretty fed up with the behaviour of the Cartwright males at the party. 'Thanks,' he said. 'I mean – thanks for everything. The party, too. I should have come over and said.'

Tim nodded, mollified, and Joanna came in, pushing a tea trolley whose cloth hung over its sides in lacy triangles. 'I didn't know whether to peel the cucumber for the sandwiches or not,' she said anxiously.

'No, you want to leave it on,' Barbie told her. 'Makes you burp if you peel it.'

Joanna looked wretched. 'Oh, dear,' she said. 'I did.'

After Barbie and Tim had left, Nick decided that he couldn't stay in the Bowman household any longer. 'It's really nice of your mother to let me come here,' he explained to Sasha, 'and I hope she won't think I'm being rude. Well – not ruder than usual. But I've got to go home sooner or later.'

Sasha nodded understandingly. 'It's just delaying the moment of having to face it,' she said. 'I do see what you mean. But I thought, yesterday – coming straight back from abroad to all that – '

'No, it was great,' Nick assured her. 'It gave me time to think.' Or at least, time to know he'd have to go back to the flat and think, he amended privately. He badly wanted to be by himself, on his own territory.

'Shall I come with you?' Sasha offered. 'Mum's going to this concert tonight, with Geoffrey.'

'Oh, the boy friend,' said Nick. 'So you'll be on your own, you mean?'

He had not intended to frown, but Sasha said quickly, 'It doesn't matter. I'm not asking to tag along or anything. I just thought – '

'Yes, I know. Sorry. I didn't mean – '

Sasha put her hands on either side of his face and kissed him. 'Let's not get into a muddle,' she said. 'It's all right. Do what you want to do.'

'Okay,' said Nick, relieved. Thank God for that, he thought.

Joanna was not quite so accommodating. 'Well, you must suit yourself, I suppose,' she said, looking piqued. 'I could have ironed those shirts for you if you'd just waited until tomorrow.'

'Honest, it doesn't matter,' Nick assured her. He had not worn an ironed shirt for years.

'No,' said Joanna. 'I didn't think it would.' But Nick noticed with relief, she didn't actually sigh. She went on rather firmly, 'I can't give you a lift home, I'm afraid. I'm going out this evening, and I have to get ready.'

'Nick, you can borrow the bike,' said Sasha suddenly. 'I can't ride it until my licence comes through, so you may as well use it.'

Nick felt a leap of the heart. 'Are you sure you don't mind?' he asked, trying to pretend that the idea was a complete surprise to him. It would have been out of line to ask her for it, but it was great that she'd offered.

'No, you're welcome,' said Sasha. 'I know you'll take care of it.'

Joanna was disapproving. 'Aren't you being a little rash?' she said. 'What about insurance and that sort of thing?'

'I'm still insured,' said Nick. 'I didn't cancel it.' That would have been admitting that he was permanently bikeless.

'There you are, then!' said Sasha with her radiant smile. 'No problem! And my crash helmet fits him.'

'Well, I suppose you know what you're doing,' her mother said. 'I must decide what to wear.' And she left the room. She was improving, Nick thought.

It was good to be on a bike again. The Honda was no great thrill, but it had enough speed to allow reasonable progress along the thinly-populated Sunday streets, and Nick enjoyed riding. The rear wheel sprocket was a fraction loose, he decided, but he could soon tidy that up.

As he turned into the street which led to the flats, he wondered what the hell he would do if this bike got stolen as well. It would be even worse, having to break the news to Sasha. He wished he could put the Honda somewhere close, where he could keep an eye on it. Then he saw the solution.

He rode across the concrete, between the pillars under the flats, and came to a stop by the lift, where he leaned from the bike to put his finger on the button. Now that Maurice was not around to object, he would take the bike up to the flat.

After some time, the lift arrived and he wheeled the 125 into its metal-lined interior. It only just fitted.

A woman got in at the walkway level and stared at the bike with distaste as she squeezed her way past it. 'What d'you think you're doing?' she demanded. 'You can't take this blooming thing upstairs.'

'Can,' said Nick.

She ranted about it all the way to the tenth floor, where she got out. 'I'll complain to the Council!' she shouted through the closing doors. 'You young yobs, it's about time someone – ' In the last of the narrowing gap, Nick help up two fingers.

He felt better with the Honda standing in the hall. Not only was the bike safe, but it made the flat seem a slightly different place. In fact, it dominated it. Although the 125 was not as big as the Kawasaki had been, it still filled up the hall almost completely, and its oily smell crept pleasantly into every room. He went into the kitchen and made a cup of coffee. There was, after all, a half-full carton of milk in the fridge. It must have been there for over a fortnight, he thought, sniffing at it cautiously – but it was UHT and didn't smell any worse than usual. He tipped some into his coffee and took the mug into the living-room. He nudged the sofa round to a different angle before he sat down on it, so that he didn't have to look at Maurice's empty chair. He would have to do something about this flat, he thought. Chuck the rubbish out. Perhaps he could get some different chairs from a second-hand shop. The main thing was to find a job, quickly. Never mind if it was tedious. He could put up with it for a bit. Maybe he could get someone to share the flat. It would help with the rent. Or could he get Housing Benefit or something? He would have to go and see the person who had written him the letter about Maurice. There was a lot he needed to know. The coffee tasted awful.

Minutes passed. It was wonderfully peaceful. Nick had a pang of guilt as he realised this, but the fact could not be denied. From now on, no voice would be raised in complaint or argument. No television programme would be switched on or off except by Nick himself. He was free to do exactly as he liked. There was something almost unnerving about it. Surely *someone* would object? But the flat's quietness made no comment. Nobody would care what Nick Cartwright did, he realised. Nobody would even know he existed, so long as he did not impinge on those other lives which made themselves known in the form of creaking footsteps from the flat above, or as water running in the pipes or a distant radio.

So this is it, Nick thought, looking round the room. Shabby furniture, walls with graffiti seeping through the paint, someone else's bike standing in the hall. This is the truth of the moment, just as lying on the hard earth in France had been the truth of another moment, or the weird meeting with the huge, warm pots in the darkness. This, now, was what he had to work with. The rest was up to him.

Feeling that it was time to take stock, he reviewed his assets.

153

At least he had a roof over his head. And his bank account, although empty, was still functioning. There was a bit of lee way yet before they shut up shop on him. He had a lot of job experience and a good line in tall stories, not to mention an appealing smile and honest-looking blue eyes. Failing all else, there was the DHSS. And there was Sasha.

But Sasha had gone out with bloody Roger.

All the time he had been in France, Nick had hardly thought about Sasha. It had seemed that he had simply left her behind, like everything else associated with London, but he knew now that he had almost deliberately kept her out of his mind. He had got into the habit of thinking that she was a bit of a drag, and travelling had provided a welcome excuse to get away from the whole thing. But she was the one person who steadily and consistently stuck up for him. She had fought her way through all his impatience and casual rudeness, past the point where all the other girls he'd known had given him up as a bad job. But Sasha was still there.

Or was she? Nick thought of her patience and kindness since yesterday, and wondered if she was only being nice to him because of Maurice. Perhaps she was just waiting until she judged that Nick was sufficiently recovered from the shock to stand on his own feet, then she would go off with Roger. Or someone. A girl who looked like that could easily find a bloke with a good job and a car and a Barrett house. Already, she was talking about having to be independent of him. Nick thought of the conversation in Kew Gardens, and wondered how he could have been so stupid. He had practically told her then to back off and leave him alone. What if she was planning to do just that? He thought of her quick smile and the cascade of crazy-coloured hair, and the mad things she made and wore. She was such a turn-on.

And he had been thinking of getting someone to share the flat. He thumped himself on the forehead. What an idiot! If he was going to share with anyone, why not Sasha? It was probably too late now. He had discouraged her too often. In a kind of panic, he went to the telephone and dialled her number.

'Hello!' she said, surprised. 'What's the matter? The bike

hasn't broken down, has it?'

'No,' said Nick. He didn't know what to say to her.

'What is it, then? Are you all right? Oh – hang on a minute.' He heard her say, 'Bye-bye, Mum. Have a lovely time. I'll see you later.' Then her voice was in his ear again. 'Nick? Sorry – I just had to say good-bye to Mum.'

'Yes.' There was a long pause. Then he said, 'I've been thinking.'

'I expect you have, love,' she said sympathetically. There was that dreadful patience in her voice, like a mother looking back to encourage a toddler who stumbled along behind her. 'Sasha,' he said. Half measures wouldn't do. She'd want the real thing. 'Will you marry me?'

He heard a breath of astonishment, then she began to laugh. He was right, he thought. She didn't care any more. She'd learned to manage without him.

'Oh, darling.' She sounded warm and amused. 'You *must* be feeling low.' Then she settled to a more serious assessment of the situation. 'I know everything's dreadful at the moment, and you're all alone there, with nothing in the fridge, but you mustn't panic.'

Blast the woman, he thought, grinding his teeth. She didn't have to be so damned condescending. How could he have let himself in for this? If she was going, see if he cared. 'A passing thought,' he said lightly. 'Temporary brainstorm.' Raking about in excuses like a cat raking the earth over what it had done, he added, 'Empty fridge, yes. I just wanted a serf to send out for some nosh. 'Spect I'd better go down the Pakistani shop.'

''Spect you had,' said Sasha. There was still a smile in her voice.

'Yeah. Well, see you.' He hung up quickly. Oh, *shit*, he thought. He grabbed his jacket and a cheque book. He bloody well would go down the Pakistani shop.

The phone was ringing when he got back with a laden carrier bag. He kicked the door shut behind him and side-stepped his way past the Honda. That would be Sasha, he thought as he reached for the receiver. He was in for another of those agonising conversations about being honest with each other and preserving independence. But it wasn't.

'Hi,' said Gary. 'You're back. I've rung a couple of times. Sorry to hear about your old man.'

'Oh. Well – one of those things, I suppose.' Nick felt disorientated. He had been so sure it would be Sasha.

'Liz sends her sympathies as well. How was France?'

'Great.'

'We're getting married on Saturday. Half-past ten, at the Registry Office. Liz says you're to be there.'

'Day after the funeral,' said Nick, more to himself than Gary. 'Yeah, okay. Sasha told me you were getting married. I've been over at hers since yesterday. I got back here in the afternoon and there was this letter about the old man, and one from her saying to give her a ring. So I did.' It was all too late. He'd blown it.

'Better than sticking around in the flat,' said Gary. 'Liz said Sasha was in an awful state when she heard about the accident. Anyone would think it was *her* father, she said. Sasha's nuts about you, you know.'

'Is she?' Fat lot Gary knew about it, Nick thought.

'Oh, yes. Listen, are you in this evening?'

'I might be,' said Nick cautiously. He didn't really want Liz and Gary round here, chattering about domestic bliss.

'You haven't got the bike back, have you?' Gary asked.

'No.'

'You'll be in, then,' he said with certainty. 'I'm coming round. There's something I want to see you about. Be there in twenty minutes or so.' He spoke to someone, then amended it. 'Ten minutes.'

'What do you mean, something you want – '

But Gary had rung off.

Mildly irritated, Nick took his shopping into the kitchen and unloaded it. Gary didn't have to be so mysterious. His life wasn't crammed with dramatic events like some TV soap opera. He'd probably bought a second-hand washing machine or something, and wanted help plumbing it in. He pushed a couple of slices of bread into the toaster and poured the old half-carton of UHT milk down the sink. Then he realised what Gary would want to say. It would be about this business of setting up a car-mending outfit at the Brents' place. Gary had probably got it on his conscience about fixing it all up behind Nick's back. Liz would have been nagging him about it. Nick shrugged, spreading his toast with jam. It didn't matter. As things were, he couldn't have messed about with some pie-in-the-sky scheme like that, anyway. What he needed now was an earner. He had just finished his toast when the doorbell rang.

Gary blinked at the sight of the Honda taking up more or less all of the hall. 'Is that yours?' he asked.

'Sasha's,' said Nick.

'You old bugger,' said Gary admiringly. 'I might have known you'd get wheels from somewhere. Come on, we're going out.'

'We're bloody not,' said Nick. 'I'm flat broke. I've just given them a cheque at the Pakistani shop, but I can't go on doing that for long or the Bank are going to want my card back.'

'Don't be a twit,' said Gary. 'Who said anything about spending money?' He had never been any good at disguising his feelings, Nick thought. He looked like a cat that had had the cream. 'Mr Brent's downstairs in his car,' he said.

'Yeah, I know all about that,' said Nick. 'You're going to set up a car service place in his funeral parlour. Sasha told me.'

'Wrong,' said Gary. 'You haven't been in that building, have you?'

'No,' said Nick. 'I've seen it from the outside, though.'

'It isn't big enough for cars,' said Gary. 'You couldn't get more than four in at a time. But it's ideal for bikes. And that's where you come in. What we want to do is set up a bike service business, catering for despatchers who've got to have a bike on the road all the time. Work evenings and weekends, and buy in a few bikes for hire, so if a bloke has a break-down you can keep him on the road while you sort his bike out. We're going to have to work like hell, specially at first. But Mr Brent reckons the money's there.'

Nick felt a leap of excitement, followed at once by the angry knowledge that it wasn't on. 'It'll take money,' he said. 'A lot of money. We'd have to set the place up — build in a bench, buy tools. A vice, angle grinder, compressor, spray-gun. Probably a milling machine. You're looking at a grand or more.'

'Peanuts,' said Gary. 'Come on — don't keep the man waiting.'

Nick checked that he had his key, and followed Gary out. 'It's not peanuts to me,' he said. They went through the balcony door and started to clatter down the stairs.

'All you've got to find is a couple of weeks' money to live on,' Gary said. 'Mr Brent's going to set the thing up to start with. After that, if the thing gets going, he's talking about cutting you in as a partner.'

'Hang on,' said Nick.

Gary paused on a half-landing and looked at him. 'I'm not coming into it full-time,' he said. 'I thought about it, but with Liz and the baby and everything, it's too much of a risk. I'll work there at weekends, to make a bit of extra money so we can get the flat set up and everything, but I'll stay at Len's.'

And in thirty years you'll be like Jim, Nick thought. It seemed sad, somehow. 'If that's what you want,' he said. They started off again down the stairs. Sasha's father was the man to ask about all this. He'd offered to try and find Nick a job, and you couldn't be much more willing than that. Even if he'd mucked things up with Sasha, she wouldn't mind him getting a word of advice from her old man. She would probably continue to take a motherly interest in his affairs.

He went on running down the stairs, trying to kill the excitement which kept bubbling up inside him. Things weren't that easy. He had always wanted to work with bikes, but the professional firms wanted time-served, qualified mechanics, or they wanted school-leavers for cheap labour. He wasn't either. But he mustn't believe in it too much, or he would be vulnerable to disappointment. He waited for Gary to catch up and said, 'What's the plan for this evening, then?'

'We'll go and have a look at the place,' said Gary, 'then have a drink and sort out what to do next.'

'Lend us a fiver, then,' said Nick. 'It's a bad start if I can't even buy the man a drink.'

With an air of resignation, Gary dug in his pocket.

It was nearly midnight by the time Nick got out of Mr Brent's Audi 100, back at the flats. He watched the car drive off and raised a hand in farewell. It had been quite an evening. The funeral parlour would make a marvellous workshop. It already had lights and power, and there was a built-in bench, dating from the days when they had made coffins in there.

Poor old Maurice, Nick thought as he walked across to the lift. The occupant of a coffin. There was something horribly neat about the way he and Nick had shifted places. A few weeks ago, Maurice had been the one who could shout and bully, and now he was nothing. He had joined the army of used-to-be people, his body dealt with by the professionals in these matters, with chapel and coffin and fire. And Nick sensed himself to be at a new beginning.

The lift came, and Nick got into it and leaned against its metal side as it quivered its way upward. This autumn had been crazy, he thought. Everything had changed. Perhaps things had always been changing, in the same way that children grew, unnoticed by anyone except the occasionally-visiting granny. A phrase of Sasha's came back to his mind. 'This is Nick's October revolution, is it?' He smiled. No, it wasn't a revolution. Things had revolted around him, robbing him of job and of father and, probably, of girl friend, but the effect of all that was to make him settle for what he was. In an army, he thought, it would be a revolution if you decided not to fight any more.

The lift arrived at the twelfth floor. He got out and started towards his balcony, hands in pockets, staring at the floor as he thought with embarrassment and regret about his phone call to Sasha earlier that night. He really had cocked the situation up now, with that stupid impulse to ask her to marry him. No wonder she had laughed.

He shouldered his way through the swing door, then stopped, astounded. Sasha, huddled like a refugee, was sitting on a large suitcase outside the door of his flat.

'I got on a bus,' she said. 'I've been here ages.' She stood up,

159

a little unsteadily, and Nick took her wordlessly in his arms. 'I'm not going to marry you,' she went on, her voice indistinct as she buried her face in his neck. 'But you didn't mean that, did you?'

'No,' said Nick. 'I thought it was what you'd want.'

'I'm sorry I laughed. It was only because I was happy.'

'Were you?' At this moment, he never wanted to let her go.

'Yes.' She looked up at him, but her smile was fleeting. 'It doesn't happen often, does it? Not being *really* happy.'

Nick did not answer. She was right. It didn't happen often. And when it did, you couldn't add to it by talking about it. With his arm still round Sasha's shoulders, he fished in his pocket for the key.